CHRISTMAS
——— ON THE ———
NILE

THE SHERLOCK HOLMES
AND LUCY JAMES MYSTERIES

THE SHERLOCK HOLMES
AND LUCY JAMES SHORT STORIES

The series page at Amazon:
amzn.to/2s9U2jW

THE **SHERLOCK HOLMES/
LUCY JAMES** MYSTERIES

CHRISTMAS
— ON THE —
NILE

BY **ANNA ELLIOTT**
AND **CHARLES VELEY**

Typesetting by FormattingExperts.com
Cover design by Todd A. Johnson

CHAPTER 1: LUCY

Piccadilly Circus was always crowded: aristocratic chariots and barouches vied for space on the road with shabby growlers and double-decker omnibuses blazoned with advertisements for Lipton Teas. And now, with Christmas only a few weeks away, the streets surrounding the Shaftesbury Memorial Fountain at the centre of the circus were even more crammed with traffic than usual.

Pedestrians hurried to and fro, laden with parcels as they rushed to buy the toys and ladies' watches and new handkerchiefs prominently displayed with boughs of holly in the shop windows. A band of French horns, flutes, oboes, and trombones had gathered on the street corner nearest the Geological Museum and were working their way doggedly through Handel's *Messiah*, despite the din of street noise. A grocer's cart had tipped over in the road, creating a snarl of carriages and curricles whose drivers—with a good many shouted oaths and insults—were trying to find a path around the blockage.

The helmeted policeman who was valiantly struggling to direct the traffic looked as though he would just as soon have given up in disgust.

Watson glanced out through the rear window of our own vehicle.

"Do you think we were followed?"

"If we were, our followers deserve an award for sheer persistence, if nothing else."

We had traversed what felt like a circuit around the whole of the city in an effort to shake off any pursuit, changed carriages more than once, and were now parked just outside the sham-antique gate of St. James's Church. I had been keeping a watch on both the cabs and the pedestrians who passed us by, but I hadn't been able to spot anyone taking more than a passing interest in our presence.

I couldn't dispel the hard knot of uneasiness inside me, though, and the fog wasn't helping. Far from offering a white Christmas, London seemed determined that its citizens would spend all of December battling the thick pea-soupers for which the city was famed. Bilious curls of yellow-green mist clung to the rooftops and drifted sullenly along the muddied streets, growing thicker by the minute.

"We'll be lucky to see our hands in front of our faces in another hour," Watson muttered.

Watson was usually an unshakable source of steady dependability and calm, but now he shifted in his seat, a deep furrow etching his brows.

"It will be all right," I said. I spoke as much to myself as I did to Watson. "Holmes has thought all of this through."

Watson, despite appearing somewhat gullible in his own written accounts of Holmes's cases, was not at all an easy man to deceive. The look he gave me now said that he was no more convinced than I was myself.

"We have had this identical conversation more than once, at the outset of one of Holmes's plans."

"And all of those have come right in the end."

Although a nasty voice in the back of my mind commented that everyone's luck had to run out eventually, and that fortune had decidedly not been on our side during the past several days.

Watson opened his mouth—likely to point that fact out—then stopped, stiffening.

A tall man dressed in a hound's-tooth cloak and deerstalker cap had just appeared through the swirling fog and was making his way towards us, coming from the direction of Hyde Park.

The man looked neither to the right nor the left, but simply plunged headlong into the oncoming traffic. The driver of one hansom cab hauled on the reins of his horse with one hand and shook the other, fist upraised, cursing the tall man soundly.

And behind the hansom, another carriage driver lost control of his animal altogether. The horse reared with a frightened whinny, then bolted, the carriage swayed dangerously—and somehow, in the confusion, the man in the deerstalker was knocked to the ground and flung under the rolling carriage wheels.

Watson sucked in a quick breath, and even I felt my pulse skitter to a momentary halt as a crowd gathered around the fallen man.

The policeman was first to bend down beside him, dragging him out of the muddied road. We were near enough that I could near the suggestions shouted out by the various onlookers.

"Get 'im to St. George's!"

"No, don't move 'im, 'e might have sommat bust up inside!"

The runaway horse and carriage were gone, vanished into

the thickening fog that shrouded Shaftesbury Avenue.

"Someone fetch a doctor!" one of the onlookers shouted out.

"There's no need." The policeman straightened up from where he'd been standing over the fallen man's body. "Poor chap's dead."

There was a collective gasp, and then one of the crowd—a young man in his thirties with dark brown skin and a tan suit—pushed his way to the front.

"I am a doctor." He spoke English clearly, but with a marked accent. "Perhaps I might be able to help. It may be that the man has only been knocked unconscious."

The policeman put his hand out to stop the newcomer. "Sorry, sir, but I can't let you—"

The young man ignored him, crouching down beside the tall man's body and reaching for one limp wrist.

Watson drew in another sharp breath and made an instinctive movement towards the door of our vehicle.

"No." I held his arm. "There's nothing we can do." Although I still had to dig my nails into my palms to quell the urge to go out there.

The man in the tan suit was now standing up. "You are correct. He has no pulse."

"I see there's an ambulance from St. George's Hospital right over there." The police constable gestured. "If someone will give me a hand, we can see he's taken to the morgue."

The dark-skinned young man had melted away, disappearing into the crowd, but a pair of beefy-looking tradesmen from amongst the rest of the onlookers stepped forward, and together they carried the fallen man.

I straightened my nurse's uniform, and Watson—dressed in

the uniform of a hospital orderly—sat up in his seat as the rear doors of our vehicle were flung open and the tall man's body was hefted inside.

The young constable who had stood directing traffic got in beside him, and the doors swung closed again in the face of the remaining gawkers outside. Watson eased himself out by way of the side door, and climbed quickly into the driver's seat.

With a flick of the reins, Watson started the four-wheeled ambulance carriage rolling at a rapid clip.

We travelled several bone-rattling miles, heading West over the rough cobblestones and through a dozen or more twists and turns—and then the formerly dead man cleared his throat and sat up with a grimace.

"Sherlock Holmes is dead; long live Sherlock Holmes." He turned to Jack, who had taken off his police constable's helmet and was watching out the rear window.

"Were we followed?"

Jack shook his head. "Not a sign of anyone. Although Farooq tried to follow for a block or two. If we're assuming that was Farooq?"

"Oh, I think so." I recalled the smooth, darkly handsome face of the man who had identified himself as a doctor.

Farooq led a group of young radical Egyptian students who called themselves the Sons of Ra, and were committed to winning independence for Egypt by any means possible, the more violent and bloody the better. Or rather, Farooq purported to lead them. Holmes's investigations had shown that Farooq was in point of fact merely a paid mercenary, a puppet who danced on the strings of a far larger—and far more ruthless and deadly—organisation than the Sons of Ra.

"I suppose we're lucky that Farooq is more proficient at extortion and inciting violence than he is at surveillance," I said.

"Indeed," Holmes agreed.

Watson had drawn the carriage to a halt, and now turned back to look at us over the driver's seat.

"That was a fraught moment, Holmes," he said, "when the fellow insisted on checking for your pulse."

Holmes made a dismissive gesture. "I must credit our enemies with having made themselves familiar with my past history. And anyone who has fabricated reports of his own death as frequently as I have done must expect yet another fatal accident to be met with some skepticism. I therefore took the precaution of applying a tight rubber tourniquet to my arm." He rolled up his sleeve, releasing the rubber band with a grimace. "Uncomfortable, but effective in suppressing the pulse in one's wrist. Now." He looked around us. "Watson, if you would be so good as to take the next left-hand turn? That will bring us to the bolt hole I have selected for today's purposes."

The safe houses, or bolt holes, which Holmes maintained across London were many and ranged from dank, filthy cellar rooms in East End tenement houses to hidden apartments in the most luxurious hotels the city could provide.

We had now passed into the suburb of Chiswick, a waterside district far enough from the centre of London that it still retained a hint of a rural flavour. To my surprise, the bolt hole Holmes had chosen for today's venture appeared to be a quaint half-timbered cottage with a thatched roof and a square of neat garden in the front, the whole surrounded by a picket fence.

If the goal was to elude and confound our enemies, we were likely to be successful. No one who knew the first thing about

Sherlock Holmes would dream of looking for him in the midst of so much snug domesticity.

"Ah, Selim has already arrived, I see." Holmes's gaze lighted on the horse and the cart—the same ones that had so nearly run him down—which were now tethered outside the cottage's front gate.

"He played his part quite well, I thought," Watson said.

Holmes swung himself down through the ambulance's rear doors. "Let us hope that our friend Farooq found his performance equally convincing."

"And that Farooq has not noticed Flynn," Lucy said.

Selim must have been waiting and watching for our arrival, because the instant Holmes alighted, the door to the cottage opened and a young man emerged.

Selim was Egyptian by birth, a handsome fellow with a head of curling, closely cropped dark hair and long-lashed dark eyes. As he came to meet Holmes now, though, I saw how strained he looked, his features tight with anxiety and his gaze shadowed.

Months ago, Selim had agreed to serve as our informant on the activities of the Sons of Ra. And a week ago, he had come to us with the unwelcome news that Farooq had begun to question his loyalties. His sister, Safiya, had been taken hostage, and Selim had been given the assignment of killing Sherlock Holmes in such a way that it could not be brought home to the Sons. Otherwise, Safiya would die.

Jack jumped down from the carriage after Holmes, then turned to offer me a hand. He had been watching me during the drive, and now gave me a searching look. "Worrying about your mother?"

"No—well, of course I am." I *was* worried about my mother.

A week ago, she and Safiya had been kidnapped and taken out of England by Lord Sonnebourne, the man who in reality gave the orders that controlled both Farooq and the Sons of Ra. The thought of where she was now and what she might be enduring was an ever-present lump of dread in my mind.

"Lord Lansdowne's got all the available ships in the British Navy out looking for them," Jack said.

"I know."

As far as we'd been able to determine, my mother and Safiya had been spirited away from London on a private yacht belonging to Mr. Ashe, the criminal bank manager who had been arrested at the close of our last case, but had vanished after being freed on bail.

The yacht must either have docked at some small coastal town, to be hastily re-named and repainted, or else they had soon changed ships. Because all the considerable resources of Lord Lansdowne—England's Secretary of State for War—had been unable to track them down.

"It's not just finding her that worries me." I looked over to where Holmes and Selim were now speaking together. "I'm afraid of the risks he might run."

Both Watson and I had seen Holmes in this state before—and no one looking at him could miss the tension that vibrated through him like a constant electric current. The air inside the Baker Street flat was thick with tobacco fumes from all the pipes he had smoked, and if he'd had more than a handful of hours' sleep since my mother had gone missing, I would be shocked. The sitting room floor was heaped even higher than usual with untidily-discarded newspapers, most of them opened to accounts of British activity in Egypt, and in particular, news of the great construction project

British engineers had undertaken at the Nile port city of Aswan.

Holmes had been particularly interested in that enterprise, though he had not said what connection it may have had with the Sons of Ra. He had been reticent, as was his habit during a case, and barely touched any food in the past days. And today, he might easily have been actually trampled by the runaway horse.

"He'll do whatever it takes," Jack said. "He's sure that Sonnebourne has something big and evil in the works."

"And he blames himself," I said quietly, "for not preventing my mother's being taken captive."

For that matter, I blamed myself, too. My mother was a grown woman, capable of making her own decisions, and she had wanted—no, *insisted*—on taking part in the investigation that had led to her kidnapping. But Holmes and I were experienced in the dangers involved in detective work, and my mother was not. I should have tried harder to persuade her not to run any risks.

As though reading my thoughts—which he probably had; Jack was every bit as skilled an observer as Holmes, and he knew me even better than my father did—Jack took my hand, joining our fingers together.

"The only one who's responsible for this is the man who gave the order for your mother to be taken prisoner."

"Lord Sonnebourne, in other words."

I'm not afraid. Those had been my mother's final words, in the hastily scribbled note to me that she had managed to hide for us to find. *I haven't the least doubt that the two of you will somehow find me.*

Jack's hand tightened around mine. "We'll find her. And

a few months from now, Sonnebourne will be just one more criminal we've put behind bars."

I drew in a breath. "Then we'd better move on to the next stage in our plan."

And hope that wherever she was, my mother was still able to face the dangers of her captivity unafraid.

CHAPTER 2: ZOE

It was raining in Brindisi. Not that Zoe was surprised. Torrential downpours had lashed their train carriage all the way through France. At the station in Nîmes, she overheard a passenger on the platform comment with morose satisfaction to one of his fellow travellers that it had been raining without stop for an entire month.

The rain had followed them through Nice, Genoa, Bologna, Ancona … and now the pale yellow stone buildings of Brindisi were wet and streaming, the cobblestone streets awash.

It was somehow ironic. She had been pursued from Milan, kidnapped from London, and brought here, straight back to Italy. Although Zoe had never been to the southern coastal city of Brindisi before. Another time, she might have been interested in the ancient churches and the Roman pillar—once one of a pair that had marked the end of the Appian Way.

And what are you going to do now? Sherlock Holmes—or her imagined version of him—commented inside her mind.

She had taken to silently conversing with Sherlock a good deal these past two weeks. It was one of the few things that had kept her from giving way to fear or blind panic throughout the long, solitary hours of their journey.

She had made the discovery that fear and tedium weren't, as she would have supposed, incompatible. It was possible to be utterly terrified and excruciatingly bored at the same time. And a very unpleasant combination the two emotions made, too.

She released a breath, answering Sherlock.

That's easy for you to say.

She stopped herself before she could add, *You're not the one who's here, being carted all across Europe like a bundle of luggage.*

Sherlock—her imagined Sherlock—would only make the same reply that the real Sherlock Holmes would probably have made, if he had been present in the room with her: that of course he wasn't here. He would have been far too intelligent to get himself taken prisoner in the first place.

Instead, Zoe looked out through the small window of the inn where they were to stay the night. The room was chilly, despite the fire that burned in the fireplace, and a gust of wind flung a spatter of water droplets against the pane of glass.

She didn't know where their journey would next take them. Her captors had been careful not to inform her of any details, even the location where they were bound.

If she knew that, she might be able to make plans, formulate some means of escape.

Zoe supposed it was flattering that they credited her with that much intelligence and capability, given that she felt as trapped as a butterfly skewered to a lepidopterist's specimen card. Even if she knew their destination, she didn't see any way—

The sound of the door opening made her break off that depressing train of thought.

She'd assumed that it would be Mrs. Orles returning, but instead it was the maidservant: a pretty, rosy-cheeked Italian girl, who curtsied and said, "The gentleman wishes to see you. Downstairs."

The gentleman. Sonnebourne.

Zoe's heart kicked hard against her ribs, but it wasn't as though she could refuse.

On the bed behind her, Safiya moaned and tossed her head restlessly on the pillow. She would be waking soon, or as close to waking as she ever came.

The bones of her face looked too sharp beneath the skin, and her breathing had an unhealthy rasp to it that Zoe didn't at all like. How long could even a healthy young girl be kept semi-starved and drugged? At the very least, all the opium Safiya had been given would be wreaking havoc on her constitution.

If they ever got out of this alive, Zoe thought grimly, Sherlock might well have to give the girl advice on recovering from the effects of a drug addiction.

But for that to happen, she needed a way to ensure that Sherlock found both of them.

And for now, Safiya's presence—and vulnerability—were a vivid reminder of exactly why Zoe had to trot meekly to obey Lord Sonnebourne's summons.

For now.

Unless she could think of some way out of here.

She made herself nod and smile at the serving girl and say, "Of course. I'll come straight away."

Fear gave your enemy power over you. She couldn't remember whether it was from Sherlock she'd heard that saying. No, on second thought, it couldn't have been him; to speak of fear would have been to admit that he was vulnerable to the human frailty of being afraid.

It was true, though. In every other regard, she was currently in Lord Sonnebourne's power. She could at least refuse to live in terror of him.

Her heart was still beating sickeningly in her ears, though, as she opened the door to the small sitting room downstairs, which Lord Sonnebourne had taken over for the duration of their stay.

He was standing at the window with his back to her, looking out to the nearby harbour, where through the rain and the sea mist, Zoe could just barely make out the outline of a steamer ship at anchor.

She was certain that he'd heard her come in, but he didn't move or acknowledge her presence. She counted off eight, then nine beats of her own heart before he swung around and said,

"Sherlock Holmes is dead."

The words struck like a slap. Zoe felt as though she were falling, as though the floor had just opened up below her. Only the knowledge that Sonnebourne was watching her closely, expecting a reaction to the blunt statement, enabled her to keep her expression neutral.

"You must be happy to hear it."

Sonnebourne was a big man, somewhere in his middle forties, tall and broad-shouldered, with a strong-boned, handsome face and light blond hair. He leaned forward a little.

"You are not distressed by the news?"

"Were you expecting that I would be?"

Sonnebourne didn't answer. Instead his eyes, startlingly blue in his tanned, leonine face, continued to bore into Zoe's.

Even now, with her pulse skipping and sickness rising in her, Zoe was conscious of the magnetic pull of his personality, the way his intense blue gaze focused on her as though she were at that moment the most important thing in his world.

A wasted effort, since she was not only his prisoner, but also knew him to be a cold-blooded murderer many times over. But she had, at that moment, been able to understand why for several years Lord Sonnebourne had been the successful leader of a cult of gullible and extremely wealthy sun worshipers. Powerful and charismatic, he looked on all the world with the intent, hypnotic gaze of a snake charmer bending his animal charge to his will.

"Or perhaps you do not believe it is true?" he asked. His voice was almost gentle.

Zoe shrugged. "If you wish to appear a trustworthy source of information, my lord, I would recommend not beginning a relationship with kidnapping and extortion. You must admit that you have so far given me no reason to believe a word that you say is true."

Deliberately provoking a homicidal lunatic might be considered a dubious strategy for survival, Holmes commented in Zoe's mind.

I'm doing the best I can.

Sonnebourne smiled—a wolfish smile, baring eye teeth—"None whatsoever, my dear Miss Rosario. However, I had a telegram this evening from my agent in London." He indicated the form on a nearby table. "Sherlock Holmes was knocked down in the street by a runaway carriage and pronounced dead on the scene."

"I see."

Zoe was still trying to let nothing of her thoughts show. But Sonnebourne, whatever his faults, was not unobservant.

"You are relieved to hear that. You suspect—as I suspect—that so mundane a death hardly fits so extraordinary a man. Therefore, one is forced to the conclusion that the accident was a fake—a trick to make me believe that the great Sherlock Holmes was no more."

He would know if she tried to lie.

Zoe said, choosing her words carefully, "It wouldn't be the first time that Sherlock falsified reports of his death."

She still remembered the cold, hollow agony that had filled her when she had read Dr. Watson's account of The Final Problem.

She hadn't, at that time, seen Sherlock in years, or allowed herself any communication with him, beyond reading Dr. Watson's stories in the newspapers. And yet the world had somehow seemed a much lonelier, emptier place without him in it.

Sonnebourne was still smiling—the only warning Zoe had for what he was about to say. "Nevertheless, I would have expected you to show more concern. Given that he is the father of your daughter."

If her heart had skipped before, it now jolted as though she had been kicked in the chest. She should have foreseen that Sonnebourne would have learned the secret of Lucy's identity. But she also knew—had known from the instant that she laid eyes on Lucy's tiny newborn face all those years ago—that she would do anything, anything at all, to protect the small, utterly perfect life that she and Sherlock had managed to produce. Even if it meant ripping her own heart to shreds in the process.

Lucy was grown up, strong and beautiful and able to defend herself, now. Zoe knew it. But in this moment, she still wanted to launch herself at Sonnebourne, tear the smug, cruel smile off his face, threaten to kill him with her bare hands if he tried to harm a single hair on Lucy's head.

Instead, she waited for her heart to stop hammering.

How much did Sonnebourne actually know, and how much was he guessing? That was the important question, the one that

Sherlock would tell her to ask herself if he were here.

Unless he really was dead.

No. She couldn't think that way. Sherlock was alive, Lucy was safe, and she, Zoe, was going to keep herself alive so that she could see both of them again.

And if she managed in the process to bring about Sonnebourne's unpleasant end, then so much the better.

"Sherlock abandoned me years ago, when he learned I was going to have a child," she said aloud.

Sonnebourne's eyebrows went up. "Indeed."

"Yes." She spoke the lie without blinking, silently apologising to Sherlock in her own mind as she said it. He would have married her, if he had known of Lucy's existence.

Sherlock might be maddening, arrogant, and as incapable of settling down to ordinary domestic life as a shark was of turning strictly vegetarian. But he was an honourable man. The choice to end their brief relationship—and not to tell him about the baby she was expecting—had been Zoe's. Because he was by nature incapable of being a husband or a family man, and Zoe had known that attempting it would only make him miserable, and herself miserable in turn.

Aloud she went on, "If you imagine that I feel any personal loyalty to him or affection for him, you are quite mistaken."

"And yet when you were threatened in Milan, you went straight to him," Sonnebourne said.

He sounded skeptical. But he hadn't contradicted anything she'd said. She was right. He might guess, but he didn't know.

Small wonder. Professor James Moriarty had gone to a great deal of trouble to ensure that no one would know the specific details surrounding Lucy's parentage and birth.

Zoe raised her eyebrows. "Do you fall in love with a hammer, simply because it is the right tool for the job when you wish to pound in a nail? I have sought Sherlock's assistance in the past because he is uniquely suited to deal with criminal matters. But that is all."

"And he feels nothing for you?" Sonnebourne asked. "That is hard to believe of so charming a lady."

He was smiling as he said it, but all the same, ice crawled across Zoe's skin and the fine hairs on the back of her neck stood on end.

She had seen lions, frustrated and angry, pacing behind the bars of their cages in the zoo. Lord Sonnebourne's eyes had precisely that look of chained, barely contained violence. He kept the violence under tight control, but she didn't doubt for a moment that he would thoroughly enjoy any opportunity she gave him to let the merciless, savage streak in his nature run free.

"Only Sherlock knows what he feels—if indeed he feels anything at all," she said. She allowed a note of bitterness to creep into her tone. It wasn't in fact difficult.

She was trying to persuade Sonnebourne that she was angry with Sherlock, resentful of him for being what he was. Fortunately, she had a good deal of experience with feeling both of those emotions.

What had Sherlock said to her in greeting back in London, after more than a year apart, and not a single letter or communication from him during all of that time? *Regrets are illogical.*

Her one tiny source of satisfaction was, oddly, the very blankness of his expression as he had said it. Surely he would not have been working quite so hard to betray no private feelings if he had not felt something at seeing her again.

"He abhors emotion and holds reason and logic above all else."

"So I have heard." Sonnebourne studied her a moment, eyes half closed, and then his teeth flashed in another wolfish grin. "If what you tell me is true, then you have no value as a hostage. I should release you—or perhaps simply kill you now?"

He was testing her—although Zoe didn't doubt that if the whim struck him, he would kill her, without any more thought or regret than he would give to squashing an insect.

Above the hammering of her heart, she said, "Not necessarily. Sherlock may not feel anything for me, personally, but I must at least credit him with a strongly altruistic streak to his nature. That is in part why he pursues his chosen profession of detective. He might decide that my death would be undesirable because of the pain it would cause Lucy. And besides, there are other ways I might be useful to you."

"Such as?"

"I know Sherlock Holmes," Zoe said. "If you are correct in your suspicions that he is still alive, then you must assume that he will be coming after you. You would be better prepared to face that danger if I can tell you how he thinks, and what course of action he is likely to choose."

"You would betray him?"

Zoe drew a breath, ordering herself to go carefully. She felt as though she were walking a tightrope, or a sword's edge.

She couldn't expect Sonnebourne to believe that she was ready to fall in with him or his plans so easily. Whatever those plans were that had brought them halfway around the globe.

So she merely said, making her voice calm, "What is there

to betray? We have no relationship, as I have been telling you. I am a realist, Lord Sonnebourne, and I would prefer not to die in the immediate future. When Sherlock abandoned me and our daughter years ago, I was forced to learn to take care of myself. That is what I am doing now, by choosing a path that I feel will best ensure my survival."

Sonnebourne studied her for what seemed an endless moment, his eyes half-lidded, his face as inscrutable as Holmes's. Zoe tried not to hold her breath. But before he could answer, the door to the parlor opened, and Mr. Morgan bustled in.

He barely acknowledged Zoe's presence with a glance before focusing on his employer. "I must speak to you. At once!"

Sonnebourne's lips compressed with annoyance at the peremptory tone. He was undoubtedly a man who liked giving orders, not taking them, and from the looks he had cast in Mr. Morgan's direction, Zoe imagined that Lord Sonnebourne viewed the barrister as roughly the equal of an insect squashed on the bottom of his shoe: bothersome, but barely worth contempt.

He ignored the barrister and turned to Zoe with another slow smile.

"Miss Zoe Rosario." His voice seemed to taste the name as much as say it. "We will have to continue our most interesting discussion at another time. I must say that I find you a surprising woman, and not at all what I had expected."

CHAPTER 3: FLYNN

Flynn looked up at the small window high above his head. Too far up to jump for it. He'd have to find a box or a packing crate or something strong enough to climb on. He started to look around the alley, which wasn't easy with all the fog drifting about. He'd been following the man who'd tried to examine Mr. Holmes—Farooq, Mr. Holmes had called him—all the way from the scene of Mr. Holmes's supposed accident. They'd fetched up here, at a small building just off the end of the Cannon Row Wharf, near Westminster Bridge.

Farooq had gone straight in through the front door—after unlocking a big, shiny lock that made Flynn question how bright this Farooq chap could be. Put a lock like that one on your front door and you might as well take out a notice in the Times, announcing that you had something worth stealing inside.

He'd watched the door awhile, but Farooq hadn't come out again. He was still in there, unless he'd climbed out a side window. And so Flynn and slipped around the back to see if he could find another way in, or at least get a look at what Farooq was hiding in there that was so valuable.

This close to the Thames, the fog was even thicker than it

was in the rest of the city, like having a soggy blanket pressed against your face. Yellow green mist was all over the towers on the Houses of Parliament, which were just down the river from here. Fog hung in the rigging of the big ships that were moored at the wharf, and Flynn could only just make out the barges and small boats that were sailing upriver and down. How the captains of the ships managed not to crash into each other was anyone's guess.

Flynn kicked at a metal bucket with the bottom gone rusty, trying to decide if it would be strong enough to hold his weight, then jumped as someone stepped towards him out of the misty shadows at the head of the alley.

"Have you found a way in yet?" Becky asked.

Flynn tried to swallow down his heart, which felt like it should have knocked up against his back teeth. Not that he should have been surprised that Becky had found him.

"I thought you were staying in Baker Street and letting Mrs. Hudson teach you how to mend socks or some such," he told her.

Mrs. Hudson had started giving Becky lessons in sewing. Flynn would have run a mile in tight boots to avoid having to learn anything of the sort, but Becky didn't mind. She said it gave her practice for when she was a doctor and had to stitch up people.

"I was," Becky said. "I mended three stockings, too. But then Mrs. Hudson fell asleep in her chair by the fire, and I didn't want to wake her. Not when she's so tired out with worrying about Mr. Holmes."

They were all worried about Mr. Holmes, and about Miss Zoe, too. But Flynn would have been willing to bet the price of a hot baked potato from a street vendor's stall that Becky hadn't thought very hard about whether or not to wake Mrs. Hudson.

"So I came out and went to Piccadilly Circus to help you follow Farooq," Becky said. "I just didn't want to get too close until now, in case Farooq looked back and saw us. Two people are always more noticeable than just one." She tilted her head back to look up at the window. "Is this the only way in?"

"The only one I've found—other than the front door."

"And Farooq is still in there?"

"That's right."

"Do you think this is where he's keeping all of the weapons?"

"Let's hope so." Otherwise this afternoon of tramping over half of London after Farooq had been a waste of shoe leather.

"We'd better get a look inside, then," Becky said.

"First we'd better make sure we don't fall straight into Farooq's lap if we do."

Becky frowned, thinking, then said, "All right. What if I go around to the front and knock on the door?"

"And you'll say what to Farooq when he answers it?" From what Flynn had heard about him, the leader of the Sons of Ra wasn't likely to invite unexpected visitors in for a cup of tea.

"I won't say anything—I won't stay to talk to him, I'll just knock and then run away. But he'll come out to see who it was, and that will give you a chance to find out whether it's safe to try and get in through the window."

"All right." Flynn had to admit it was more sensible than a lot of Becky's schemes. "Give me a minute to get up there."

The rusted pail wasn't strong enough to hold him, but he'd spotted a hefty piece of lumber, more than long enough to reach from one side of the narrow alley to the other. He leaned the board up against the back wall, so that one end was braced against the building behind Farooq's, and the other end stopped just under the window.

Becky eyed the arrangement. "Don't fall."

"Thanks for the advice."

The board *did* wobble, but by the time Becky had vanished around the side of the building, Flynn had managed to crawl up on hands and knees so that his head was on a level with the window pane.

He couldn't see much, since the room inside was even darker than it was out here in the fog. But at least no one shouted at him to get down—or worse.

The building wasn't too big. Flynn's guess was that it had once been a counting house belonging to a merchant or one of the shipping firms that did business at the wharf here. It was starting to look a bit tumbled-down now, as if it had stood empty for some time before Farooq took charge. The inside of the window had cobwebs stretched across it, and now that Flynn was closer to the roof, he could see that it was missing tiles in spots.

But more important, now that his eyes had adjusted, he was pretty sure that there were at least two rooms inside, and that the one he was looking into was a small back room. Across from the window, he could see a door—which was pulled tight shut—and stacks of crates on the floor.

From around the front, he heard Becky's knocking, and drew in his breath. *Nothing ventured, nothing gained.*

He'd heard Dr. Watson say that once, and it had struck him as a neat way of putting it. A bit flowery, maybe, but then Dr. Watson was an author and liked to use big words.

He dug his pen knife out of his pocket and wedged the blade under the catch on the window. It was as old and worn as the rest of the building, and snapped up with barely any effort. Flynn shoved the window up and scrambled inside, hanging by his hands from the windowsill so that he could drop to the ground with as little noise as possible.

He still made a thump, and he froze, listening. He didn't hear any voices, which was good. Becky must have kept her promise about not hanging about to talk to Farooq when he came to the door.

But then, a second later, he heard something else: footsteps, from outside the room, but coming closer.

Flynn's pulse hammered and he tried to think out what he was going to say if—*when*—Farooq or someone else walked through the door. That was, if he got a chance to say anything, and whoever found him didn't just greet him with a bullet to the head.

He'd already seen the words stamped on the crates in here: *Mauser. Gewehr 98.* Guns, all of them. But at least the wooden crates offered some cover. Flynn ducked down behind a pile and plastered himself to the floor, holding his breath. The hiding place wasn't going to be much good if Farooq decided to have a good look at all his nice new toys here, but it was the best he could do.

He heard the sound of the doorknob turning, and he shut his eyes, wondering if it would do any good if he prayed that Becky would decide to knock on the front door again.

A voice called out from somewhere in the front room.

Not Becky. The voice was a man's, and it said something in Arabic. Something with *Marhaba* in it. Flynn knew from his talks with his friend the Persian artist that meant *Hello*.

The knob stopped turning, the footsteps went away again, and Flynn breathed out. Maybe there was something to this prayer business after all.

CHAPTER 4: ZOE

Mr. Morgan and Lord Sonnebourne were arguing. The room she shared with Safiya was directly above the downstairs parlour, and Zoe could hear their voices from below.

Her heart quickened. The men's voices were rising. And more importantly, Mrs. Orles was still downstairs, gone to use the inn's bathing chamber to wash off the stains of travel.

Zoe listened for a moment for the sounds of footsteps on the steps leading to their room, and when she heard nothing, she pushed back the woollen rug that covered the floor and lay down, pressing her ear against the bare wooden boards.

The men's voices came through, the sound muffled but the words clear:

"This is an unnecessary and foolish risk!"

That was Mr. Morgan speaking, his voice high with exasperation.

He was older than Lord Sonnebourne, as well as smaller than his lordship, and running to fat, with grey hair combed forwards to cover not nearly enough of his otherwise bald head.

Zoe supposed she ought to credit him with courage for standing up to his employer, if nothing else.

"I left everything—gave up everything—to come with you!" Morgan went on. "I demand—"

"Demand?" Sonnebourne's voice hadn't risen; indeed, Zoe had to press her ear closer to the floorboards to hear it. But his tone still made an involuntary shiver run the length of her spine.

She pictured Morgan swallowing convulsively; certainly his voice sounded husky as he continued, "There may be a battalion of British soldiers waiting for us at the dock."

"If so, we shall receive a warning when we reach Tripoli," Sonnebourne replied, "and we can change our course accordingly."

Tripoli. That was at least a definite name of a city. But obviously not their final destination. Zoe shut her eyes, wishing that she could reach through the floorboards and drag the information she wanted to know out of the men below.

How much longer did she have before Mrs. Orles finished bathing and came upstairs?

"Is that telegram from London?" Morgan asked.

"Yes. Holmes is dead. Or so he would have us believe. The Egyptian girl's brother demands her release."

From the sound of his voice, Sonnebourne was smiling.

Morgan snorted. "And you mean to comply?"

"Clearly not."

Morgan grunted. "I still say we should kill her. It is a confounded nuisance carrying her about, keeping her drugged in this way. And by the time her brother learned of her death, our operations in London would already have come off. We could drop her body in the harbour, where it would not be found until we were well away—"

Zoe ignored the qualm of sickness that sprouted in her stomach at the sound of Morgan's growing enthusiasm for the plan.

Alistair Morgan might not frighten her as much as Lord Sonnebourne. But he was like one of the lower-ranked wolves that snarls and whines and cringes around the alpha of the pack: contemptible, but no less dangerous for all of that. And he certainly shared one characteristic with his employer: an utter disregard for human lives other than his own.

"Enough." Sonnebourne cut Morgan off shortly.

"But she has no further value—"

"She does have value. Value to me." Sonnebourne's voice sounded almost purring as he went on. "I hope you do not imagine that because I have allowed you to accompany me on this journey, you are privy to all of my plans? Or that you are in any way essential to them?"

"No … that is, yes … I mean—" Morgan sounded flustered now, and more than a little afraid.

As well he might. If Zoe was certain that Sonnebourne had no particular regard for her own life except for the leverage it gave him over Holmes, she was equally certain that he would dispose of Mr. Morgan just as easily and without regret if it suited him.

She'd read Sherlock's files on Sonnebourne in London, at the start of all of this. Those who cast their lot with his lordship tended to drastically reduce their life expectancies.

"Good. I have booked our passage on one of the steam freighters at anchor in the harbour," Sonnebourne said. "It will stop in Tunisia, then in Libya—"

Zoe heard the creak of a footstep on the stairs and her pulse skipped.

Please, please.

"—then in Alexandria," Sonnebourne went on. "And from there, we will travel by rail to—"

The floorboards on the landing outside the door creaked.

Zoe jumped up, kicked the rug back into place, and was sitting calmly on her own bed when the door opened.

But she'd had just barely enough time to catch Sonnebourne's final words: *to Cairo.*

CHAPTER 5: ZOE

The same red-cheeked serving girl was clearing the supper things away from their small table.

"Per favore!" Zoe caught the girl's attention before she could turn to the door.

Safiya had eaten a few mouthfuls, then almost collapsed face first into her plate of lamb stew. She would have slid straight off her chair and onto the floor if Zoe hadn't been there to catch her and help her back to the narrow bed where she now slept.

For the first few days of their journey, Zoe had kept a close watch on the young Egyptian girl who was an unwitting hostage to her own good behaviour. If she could find a chance of speaking to Safiya ... if the two of them could form some plan of escape ...

But Zoe had long since given up that idea. Mrs. Orles and Mr. Morgan saw to it between them that Safiya was dosed with enough opium powder to keep her drowsy and compliant. She slept almost all of the time, although they had to let her wake occasionally to eat and drink.

But on those occasions, the Egyptian girl merely chewed her food and drank from her cup like one in a trance, then fell back asleep again. Zoe wasn't even sure that Safiya spoke English—she certainly didn't understand any Italian—and she was even more helpless than Zoe was currently. Assistance from her was impossible.

Once you have eliminated the impossible, commented Sherlock, whatever remains, *however improbable, must be the solution.*

Zoe refrained from commenting sourly that again, that was easy for him to say. At the moment, she needed all the advice and encouragement she could get, even if it was only from a figment of her own imagination. Because she could think of very few things as improbable as the success of the scheme she had in mind.

She spoke to the serving girl in rapid Italian. "Per favore, aspetta solo un momento!"

Please, wait just a moment.

Her one slight advantage over her captors was the fact that, being Italian by birth, she spoke the language far better than they did.

The serving girl looked at her in surprise. She was young—no more than seventeen or eighteen, but Zoe thought the girl looked reasonably intelligent. And she certainly kept the rooms of the inn scrupulously clean. Zoe had already seen under the room's two beds, and there wasn't so much as a particle of dust on the bare oak floorboards.

"Come ti chiami?" she asked the girl. *What is your name?*

The girl looked still more surprised that Zoe had bothered to ask, but she said, "Valentina, Senora."

"Please, then, Valentina, I need to send a telegram."

"A telegram?" Valentina's brows wrinkled.

"Yes. There is a telegraph office nearby?" Zoe asked. There must be. Brindisi, as a busy port city, had ships from all over the globe sailing in and out of its harbour every day, bringing business that necessitated communication with the rest of the world.

The girl bobbed her head. "Yes, at the post office."

"Good." Zoe let out her breath.

She had another slight advantage in that Mrs. Orles, Mr. Morgan's former housekeeper, was no happier in her role as jailer than Zoe was to have her as a constant guard and watch dog.

Fear of Lord Sonnebourne kept her from outright abandoning her duties, but she took every possible opportunity to slip away for a few moments.

At the moment, she was out purchasing food for tomorrow's journey, since the rations aboard the freight steamer were unlikely to meet with either her own or Lord Sonnebourne's standards.

And if Mr. Morgan took it into his head to come upstairs and check on them during Mrs. Orles' absence? Or if Lord Sonnebourne decided to come and continue what he had termed their most interesting discussion?

Because she was trying to keep up her courage, Zoe snapped that thought off before it could take root.

"I'll give you the message I want to send," she told Valentina. "I have it all written out here."

She took out the message, which she had scribbled down on the paper wrapping she'd taken from a cake of soap during her own far too brief turn in the bath.

She had a single lira coin, too, which she had managed to extract from Mrs. Orles's purse.

"Will you take this to the telegraph office and see that it is sent? You can keep any change for yourself," Zoe added.

"Of course, Signora. I will see to it at once." Valentina bobbed her head and flashed a smile, showing straight, even white teeth. "Grazie."

"Thank you." Zoe let out the breath she had been holding.

Just as the door opened, and Mrs. Orles stepped into the room.

CHAPTER 6: ZOE

Mrs. Orles looked from Valentina to Zoe, her eyes narrowed.

In story books, housekeepers were plump, matronly, comfortable souls with pleasant, motherly faces. Like Mrs. Reynolds, in Miss Austen's Pride and Prejudice.

Or to choose a real-life example, like Mrs. Hudson.

Zoe had to banish that thought, because remembering anyone or anything to do with Baker Street right now felt like being stabbed with a sharp skewer. She would have sacrificed her Stradivarius to be able to instantly transport herself back to 221B.

Mrs. Orles, though, was young—in her early twenties at the most—with softly curling blond hair and a delicate, heart-shaped face.

Any outside observer would consider Mr. Morgan's former housekeeper loveliness personified. But Zoe had ample time in the course of their journey to observe the lines of bad temper and selfishness that marked the corners of her mouth, and the icy coldness of her blue eyes.

Now Mrs. Orles's eyes narrowed further as she eyed the paper in Valentina's hand. Her lips, though, curved slightly upwards in an involuntary smile.

Mrs. Orles was delighted to have caught Zoe doing something for which she could be punished.

"Give that to me!" she snapped.

She spoke in English, but her extended hand made her meaning plain.

Valentina's ready smile faded, and she looked in confusion from Zoe to Mrs. Orles.

"At once, I say!" Mrs. Orles tapped her foot in impatience. "Rapidamente!"

Looking worried now, Valentina put the message into Mrs. Orles hand.

"Now go! Partire!" The housekeeper pointed to the door.

The girl cast a quick, frightened glance at Zoe. Stupidity *was* in fact one of Mrs. Orles' flaws; she had just managed to alert the maidservant to the fact that there was something wrong about their group of travellers.

That didn't mean that Zoe wanted the girl dragged into it, though. She summoned up a reassuring smile. "Va tutto bene." *It's all right.*

Valentina still looked doubtful, but she bobbed a curtsy and went out. In ominous silence, Mrs. Orles read the message Zoe had scribbled down.

The package has been delivered to Brindisi and will be sent on to Cairo.

Another beat of silence passed, then another, and finally Mrs. Orles looked up.

She was still smiling, the faint, venomous smile that made her look like a poisoned tea cake: all loveliness and pink and white frosting on the outside, and all viciousness and spite within.

"Mr. Morgan warned you at the start of this journey what

would happen if you made any efforts to escape," she said. Her voice, too, was high and over-sweet. Her cold glance flicked to where Safiya lay deep in her drugged stupor on the bed.

Mr. Morgan had informed Zoe that any attempt to escape on Zoe's part would mean that Safiya died. Zoe hadn't doubted for a moment that he meant it.

Zoe's heart was pounding so hard that it made her feel slightly sick. But she met Mrs. Orles' gaze with a level look.

Sonnebourne might frighten her—nearly as much as Professor James Moriarty had, once upon a time. But she had met and dealt with far more intimidating villains than Mrs. Orles in her life.

"Touch her—or breathe one word of this to either Mr. Morgan or Lord Sonnebourne," she told the younger woman, "And I'll tell Mr. Morgan what actually happened to his gold and silver shaving kit that you claimed must have been stolen by a customs official."

The housekeeper's vacuously pretty face blanched, the skin around her eyes tightening.

At the outset of their journey, Zoe had wondered whether there was some sort of romantic involvement between the house-keeper and her employer. Or perhaps between Mrs. Orles and Lord Sonnebourne?

But a few days had made it clear that the relationship between Mrs. Orles and the two men was purely a business arrangement. And one didn't have to look particularly hard to understand Mrs. Orles's motivation.

Zoe had watched the younger woman counting over the coins in her reticule—and had seen her late at night, stroking the gold handle of Mr. Morgan's shaving brush, which was now safely hidden at the bottom of her own trunk.

Mrs. Orles liked money. She liked it a good deal.

Now her eyes met Zoe's for a long moment. Zoe held her breath while remaining outwardly calm, and finally the house-keeper's eyelashes fluttered and she dropped her gaze.

"Well." Mrs. Orles ripped the paper with Zoe's message in half, crossed the two halves, and ripped them all in half again before throwing them into the fire that burned in the grate. "Well," she said again. She sniffed and drew herself up, clearly attempting to regain the authority she had just lost. "Since the message is now destroyed, I do not believe there is any need to inform either of the gentlemen. But I shall be watching you, and you had better be sure that nothing of this kind happens again!"

Zoe bowed her head without a word and sat down on the edge of the bed opposite Safiya's. The scraps of her message caught fire, turned black, and shrivelled into nothing but a few wisps of ash.

Mrs. Orles watched her for what felt like an eternity, then with a final sniff, turned on her heel and went out. Zoe heard the key scrape in the lock on the door, then the sounds of Mrs. Orles entering her own small bedchamber next door and making ready to go to bed.

She shut her eyes for a moment and lay back, a wash of relief so intense it was almost painful sweeping through her. Mrs. Orles had come in at precisely the right moment to catch her in the act of making that rather obvious attempt to get a message through to Sherlock.

Now all Zoe had to do was get through the next eight hours or so until they left the inn—and pray with every scrap of faith left in her that it wouldn't occur to Mrs. Orles to look for another message, the real message, which she had already hidden under the bed for Valentina to find when she swept out the room in the morning.

CHAPTER 7: WATSON

Holmes and I were staying in the country cottage safe house. Returning to Baker Street was not possible at the time, since it would reveal to Farooq and thus Sonnebourne that Holmes was, in fact, still alive. Jack and Lucy had taken Becky back home with them. Flynn had stayed behind to make his report.

"And you overheard nothing of the conversation between Farooq and the other man?" Holmes asked.

Flynn shook his head. "They talked Arabic the whole time. I heard Farooq say something about"—he screwed up his forehead in an effort of remembrance, pronouncing the unfamiliar words carefully—"*alshahr alqadim*? He said that a couple of times."

"Next month, in Arabic," Holmes murmured. He was seated by the hearth, his fingers steepled. "Although it begs the question of whether our friend Farooq was referring to the Gregorian or the Rumi calendar, used by the Ottoman Turks."

"And he said *mayit* a couple of times, too," Flynn added. "That means, dead, doesn't it?"

"It does." A fleeting smile traced the corners of Holmes' mouth. "It is gratifying to hear that our ruse this afternoon was successful. Assuming that he was speaking of me as the individual who had shuffled off this mortal coil. You can recall nothing else?"

Flynn frowned again, but finally shook his head. "'Fraid not. Sorry, Mr. Holmes."

"You are not to blame. You did well to overhear as much as you did—and to successfully follow Farooq to his cache of weapons."

"I got a look at the fellow, too," Flynn offered. "The one who met with Farooq, I mean. Since I couldn't understand what they were saying anyhow, I climbed back out through the window and hung around the front of the building till they came out again."

To judge by Holmes' expression, he was aware that Flynn had taken a risk, but was forbearing to mention it. "And you saw the man's face? Well enough that you would recognise him again?"

Flynn's brow furrowed. "It was dark, and I couldn't get too close a look at him. But I reckon I'd know him if I saw him again. He wasn't Egyptian, that much I can tell you."

"Not Egyptian?" Holmes eyebrows edged up. "Turkish, then?"

"I don't think so," Flynn said. "He was a big chap, and he had blond hair. That much I can tell you. He wasn't wearing a hat, and I could see the colour of his hair in the street lights. Looked like maybe he'd been a fighter sometime, I'd say. Got his nose broken a time or two, from the looks of him."

"A German, do you suppose?" I asked Holmes. "We know that Farooq and his fellows have connections to the Kaiser."

Holmes' expression was particularly enigmatic. "Time will tell. Here you are, Flynn." Holmes dug in his pocket and produced a half sovereign coin, which he handed over to the boy. "I hope you will buy a hot meal and find a bed for the night."

Like myself, Holmes knew that it would be useless to offer to let Flynn stay the night here, whether on the sofa or in one of the spare bedrooms upstairs. Unless the weather was truly frigid, Flynn much preferred the open air to sleeping indoors, and abhorred all suggestions that he might accept any kind of settled domestic arrangement.

I sometimes suspected Holmes of having a sneaking sympathy with the lad's feelings on the matter. Certainly Mrs. Hudson would agree that Holmes—with his bullets in the wall, his slipper full of shag tobacco, and his mountains of papers everywhere—had a distinctly odd sense of what constituted a proper home.

"Right you are, Mr. Holmes." Flynn touched the brim of his cap, pocketed the coin, and went out.

"What are we to do about the cache of weapons?" I asked, when Flynn had gone. "Shall we inform the police, so that the weapons may be confiscated?"

Holmes was staring into the fire, his gaze abstracted, his mouth etched with a grim look. Slowly, he shook his head. "Not yet. If we—or rather the police—confiscate the weapons belonging to the Sons of Ra, their loss will be discovered by Farooq. And inevitably, word will be passed on to Lord Sonnebourne that his plans have been disrupted."

"Which would put Zoe in danger," I said. "You believe that Sonnebourne accompanied her and Morgan on the boat that left England?"

"I find it the most likely scenario. Wherever he is, Sonnebourne is assuredly not in England. Mycroft's intelligence networks would have heard by now if he were still on British soil, no matter how well hidden."

"And if Sonnebourne discovers that you have already interfered with whatever he plans to accomplish with Farooq and the others' aid, he may decide that Zoe is no longer of value to him as a hostage."

Or he might—God forbid—decide that Zoe's death was a fitting punishment for Holmes' interference. I did not voice the thought aloud, but I had no doubt that Holmes' agile mind had already leapt to foresee that possible outcome.

"It is not merely Zoe's safety which concerns me," Holmes said. I thought his tone altered, slightly, at the mention of her name, but I knew better than to expect that he would voice his fears for her aloud. I had in the past seen Holmes drive himself to a similar state—not eating, scarcely sleeping, bent on his quest to bring a criminal to justice. The stakes in the past had never been quite so high as they were now. But now, as then, my role was to offer what friendship and support I could.

"Sonnebourne is planning something," Holmes went on. "Some larger scheme, of which the Sons of Ra are only a part."

"If what Flynn overheard about the mention of next month is true, then the plans would seem likely to come to fruition sometime in the New Year," I said. "Although that is disturbingly vague."

"As you say. We must hope that Selim—having proved his worth by successfully running me down—may be admitted to Farooq's confidences and learn something more concrete of what is planned. But that unfortunately will take time." Holmes's long, mobile fingers beat an impatient tattoo on the arm of his chair. "If we could only know of a certainty where Sonnebourne has gone—"

He broke off at the shrill ring of the telephone's bell from the hall outside our sitting room. I knew that Holmes had chosen this location for our enforced period of hiding in part because of its ready means of communication with the outside world.

Only Mycroft, though, had been informed of the telephone number here.

It seemed a long time indeed that I waited for Holmes' return, anxious as to whether Mycroft's call portended good news or bad.

When he returned, Holmes' expression was still grim, but his gray eyes were alight with a focused intensity I had not seen in some time. It was the look of a hound who has at long last caught the scent of prey.

"How do you fancy a Christmas spent on the Nile, Watson?"

Accustomed though I was to Holmes' ways, I still felt my jaw go slightly slack. "The Nile? Do you mean—"

"That telephone call was from Mycroft," Holmes said. "He received a communication from Zoe, which she succeeded in getting past her captors. They are currently in Brindisi, about to board a ship which will take them to Alexandria."

"And Lord Sonnebourne?"

"Is present, as well."

"Then Sonnebourne's future plans involve Egypt."

"And are intricate and important enough to require his own presence in that country." Holmes' gaze unfocused, as though he were speculating on what those plans might be, then sharpened again. "We are limited in what we can accomplish here in London, since any active role I play in our investigation risks Farooq and his fellows discovering that my death was nothing but a sham. In Egypt, however, I will have a freer hand.

And—" Holmes's tone hardened in a way that I fancied would have laid a cold hand on even Sonnebourne's heart, had he heard it. "I confess that I would very much enjoy taking a personal hand in Lord Sonnebourne's capture."

CHAPTER 8: WATSON

The time was just before noon, shortly after we arrived in Cairo. Our carriage was stopping in line with several others at the front entrance of Shepheard's Hotel. The warm, clear daylight would normally have been welcome, but it made the two of us very visible, and the steps leading up to the hotel lobby went directly through Shepheard's famous front terrace.

"I'll keep my gaze down, and look as weary as I can," Lucy said, as she stepped down from the carriage.

At the terrace tables on either side of the steps, hundreds of hotel guests were taking their lunch or their late breakfasts, amusing themselves by observing the passers-by on the pavement below, and paying special attention to those who might be entering the hotel.

Holmes, being officially deceased, was not travelling with us, nor did I know whether he had arrived in Egypt already or had taken a later train than ours. With characteristic unwillingness to disclose any but the bare minimum of information, he had said merely that he would make his own travel arrangements, and would find a way to communicate with us once we had arrived in Cairo.

Lucy and I were travelling under our own names, but presenting the appearance of a middle-aged English gentleman with his young ward, fleeing London to escape the winter weather which now held London in its chilly grasp, and coming to Egypt for a journey up the Nile. Hundreds of Britishers and Americans did just that every year, and we hoped to blend in as merely two more ordinary pleasure travellers arriving at the beginning of the high season.

At least that was our plan.

It had been a dictum of my time in her Majesty's army that no plan survives first contact with the enemy. The past twenty-odd years had taught me that the aphorism applied equally well to life in association with Sherlock Holmes.

Lucy and I were moving quickly across the lobby in Shepheard's—for many of the leisure-seeking guests had nothing better with which to occupy themselves than to observe their fellow travellers and gossip about them—when I heard a familiar voice calling to me.

"Watson, old fellow! And Miss Lucy! Or should I say, Mrs. Kelly! What brings you to Cairo?"

My heart sank as I turned and recognised Paul Archer, an old school friend who was conducting medical research at the London Zoo when we had last seen him.

Though shy and withdrawn by nature, Paul always attracted attention, simply by his wobbly gait, the effect of a childhood case of rickets. When last we met, he had also been sickly and nerve-wracked, due to poison being slowly administered by his wife.

Now, his features framed by his rumpled straw-coloured hair, he looked tanned and fit and happy—a fact which under any other circumstances than these I would have been delighted to observe.

As it was, however, Paul had just shouted out my name and was walking briskly across the lobby towards Lucy and me, at the precise moment when I had needed our arrival to pass unnoticed.

There was no choice. I advanced towards him and shook his hand, easing him away from the registry desk and keeping my voice low, in the hopes that he would not call out my name again. "Old friend, you are looking quite well indeed," I said.

Then in a lower voice, I said, "Actually, Lucy and I are travelling incognito. We are on a case."

His eyes widened. "Terribly sorry—"

"It's fine," I said, steering him towards a quiet spot. "I don't think any harm's come of it. And of course, you had no way of knowing."

Lucy joined us. "What brings you here, Mr. Archer?"

"Oh, I'm still riding my usual hobbyhorse. Travelling alone these days. I'm here collecting specimens. Did you know Egypt has forty-seven different poisonous—"

"Thanks, old fellow," I said. "You must tell me all about it after Lucy and I have settled in to our rooms. As you can see, we've only just arrived."

Archer, though, kept speaking as though he had not heard me—as very likely he had not. He seldom had any attention to spare when engaged in conversation about his pet topic.

"It was the most extraordinary opportunity!" he went on. "About two months ago, a German chap—a doctor—named Olfrig—read one of my papers on the production of antivenin and wrote to me—"

My further attempt to cut off the flow of Archer's words died in my throat, and Lucy stared.

"Do you mean Dr. Clovis Olfrig? Of Bad Homburg, Germany?" I finally asked.

"Yes," Archer beamed. "Of course, I ought to have realised that you might know him. Fellow medicos and all of that."

A qualm that all was perhaps not as it should be appeared to be creeping in on Archer, for he gave me an anxious look.

"Is something wrong?"

I gathered my wits about me once again. "Not at all. What exactly about your research was of interest to Dr. Olfrig?"

"It concerned the varieties of Egyptian vipers. Olfrig had heard the rumours that rebellion was likely to occur in Egypt. He surmised that British troops might be subjected to poison-tipped arrows or spear points from the Egyptian rebels, and that an antivenin would be in great demand were that to occur. He wished to fund the project and share equally in the profits. If the research is successful and the British government purchases whatever antivenin is produced as a result, those profits could be considerable."

"And he brought you all this way to Egypt?" Lucy asked. "Why not simply order the snakes and have them shipped to London?"

"It is necessary for the snakes to be properly authenticated in order that the research be convincing enough to attract support from the military. And of course"—Archer gave me a half-shamed, half-boyish smile—"I could not resist the opportunity for adventure that such a trip presented! Egypt! The land of the pharaohs!"

My agreement rang somewhat hollow in my own ears, but

Archer appeared not to suspect anything amiss.

"Perhaps we might have tea later?" he asked.

"Certainly. And," I added, "I should enjoy meeting with Dr. Olfrig, as well, if that is possible."

Lucy gave me a swift, worried look, and seemed to be on the verge of speaking.

But Archer beamed once again. "Nothing easier, my dear fellow. He will be attending a fundraiser at the Cairo Museum this afternoon. We can attend together and take tea together after."

"Splendid."

We bid Archer farewell and he moved off, threading his way through the potted palm trees that ornamented the lobby.

"Are you certain this is wise?" Lucy asked when he had gone.

"I am certain, at least, that this cannot be a coincidence."

"No," Lucy agreed. "Meeting with Mr. Archer might—possibly—have been mere happenstance. But that he should have been brought here by Dr. Olfrig of all people—"

"Precisely."

I was endeavouring not to recall the time I had spent in Bad Homburg as Dr. Olfrig's prisoner.

"We must inform Holmes of this," I said. "Wherever he may be, and whenever he finds it possible to get in touch."

"I think he has done that already," Lucy said.

In response to my startled look, she tapped the open book of the hotel register, indicating a name a few lines up from the last entry: *Captain Basil*. And instead of one of the far-flung foreign locations common to the other entries, the address given was a street in Cairo: a place in the Khan Khaleel, which according to my Baedeker's guidebook was the gold and silversmith's bazaar.

"Captain Basil was the name Holmes used in the Black Peter affair," Lucy said.

I remembered the case well, though it was not one of which I had yet made a written account. In the year 1895, a former whale fisher nicknamed "Black Peter" by his crew because of his dark moods, had been murdered in his garden shed, stabbed through the chest by a harpoon.

Holmes had taken on the persona of Captain Basil in order to trap the murderer into a confession.

"Apparently Holmes wishes us to proceed to the Khan Khaleel," I said.

"Yes." Lucy was still looking in the direction that Archer had gone, a frown marring the smoothness of her brow. "Do you think it possible that Mr. Archer has turned traitor? Joined forces with Sonnebourne and through him the Kaiser?"

Since Dr. Olfrig was a known agent of the German ruler, the same terrible possibility had occurred to me. But I shook my head. "If Paul were in league with them, he would not have greeted us so openly. I think it far more likely that he is an unwitting dupe in whatever scheme Sonnebourne is planning."

"That implies two things." Lucy had gone a trifle pale, but she spoke steadily. "First, that Sonnebourne—working with Olfrig—knew that we would be arriving in Cairo, and deliberately brought Archer here to toy with us. And second, that they knew Archer to be a friend of yours, and chose him as a cat's paw in their plan simply because he *is* our known associate. Because it amuses Sonnebourne to put people that we care about in peril."

She was thinking of her mother as well as Archer, I was certain of it. "Yes." I could feel the shock I'd felt at sight of Archer solidifying into hard, cold anger. "I am quite looking forward to meeting Dr. Olfrig again this afternoon and asking him for an explanation."

"Asking? Are you sure you don't mean demanding?" A very slight smile touched the corners of Lucy's mouth, but vanished at once as she went on, "We will see Dr. Olfrig. But first the Khan Khaleel and Holmes. Because if what we surmise is true, then anyone—anyone at all—who has associated with us in any way may be in danger from Sonnebourne."

CHAPTER 9: FLYNN

Flynn pulled the edges of his jacket closer together and watched the entrance to the alley—or rather, the spot where he knew the alley started. Like everything else in London, the street across from him was so covered with yellowish-green fog that he couldn't see much of anything for sure.

Even the gin palace that stood next to the alleyway was blurry, the lamps above the door just blobs of light in the dark. From time to time, a customer came reeling out, clearly drunk, and was almost immediately swallowed up by the pea souper.

The fog made Flynn's eyes sting and his throat burn, but in a way, it was still a piece of luck for anyone wanting to take on surveillance work. In this weather, he was pretty sure he could have had a whole team of trained circus monkeys with him, and the men inside the house he was watching wouldn't have taken any notice.

More than an hour ago, he'd seen Selim go inside, along with a lot of other young men.

Flynn shifted his weight and wondered what was happening in the meeting that was taking so long. But then he heard voices, coming towards him through the fog. He pushed off from the building behind him and crossed the road.

The Sons of Ra left the meeting house mostly in groups of two and three. Flynn didn't think he recognised Selim among them, but just to be sure, he darted forward, approaching the men as they came out of the alley.

"Buy a paper, gov?" He held out the bag of newspapers he had slung over his shoulder. "Paper?"

If any of the men had actually bought a paper from him, they'd have found out that these were yesterday's editions, which Flynn had pinched off a rubbish heap. But he didn't have any takers. The men all shook their heads, muttered something—sometimes in English, sometimes Arabic—and hurried past, shoulders hunched against the drizzle of rain that had started to fall.

Selim still hadn't come out of the alley like the others, though.

Flynn took a breath, debated, then plunged towards the door he knew was halfway down the side of the meeting house building. If Selim had left some other way, he was going to have to admit that tonight had been a waste of time, and go back to watching the cache of weapons down by the river. But if Selim was still inside—

He'd almost reached the door when he heard voices.

"—but I only asked when we could expect to make our move!"

Flynn froze, his heart thudding against his rib cage. That was Selim talking.

The voice that answered him was lower pitched, and one Flynn had heard before, when he'd been crouching in amongst the crates holding guns.

"And why should you wish to know that?"

"How can you ask that? Because I desire liberty for our country, as we all do?"

"Is that so?" Farooq's voice had a silky sound to it now. "Or is it because you wish to know our plans so that you can betray us?"

"I would never do such a thing! I am loyal! But surely the longer we leave the weapons where you have hidden them, the greater the risk that they may be discovered before it is time to act—"

"The guns and ammunition are all very well." Farooq spoke brusquely. "But I have something even better—something that will make these dogs of Englishmen sit up and take notice. And it is in a safe place, where no one—not even the English police—will think of looking."

"What do you mean?"

Instead of answering the question, there was the sound of a footstep from inside, as though Farooq had just taken a step towards Selim. "As proof of this loyalty you swear, you claim to have successfully assassinated Mr. Sherlock Holmes," he said. His voice had a growl to it that sent a shiver down Flynn's spine.

"You know I did!" Selim's voice rose. "You saw the body yourself!"

"So you would have me believe. However, I have friends who are able to make inquiries into such matters, and they have discovered something strange. On the afternoon in question, no victim of a street accident was brought into either St. George's hospital or to the mortuary in Horseferry Road."

"Why would they bring him to the hospital? He was already dead!" Selim wasn't a very good liar, Flynn thought. He was probably trying to sound convincing, but his voice had a desperate ring to it. "As for the mortuary, perhaps he was taken to another. There must be many throughout the city—"

"You lie!" Farooq's voice rose to a shout, and Flynn heard a meaty kind of thump.

He knew that noise. It was the sound someone's fist made when it was driven hard into someone else's gut.

"I did not lie! I swear it! Would I risk my own sister's life—" Selim's voice rose, too, then cut off with a half grunt, half groan. Farooq must have hit him again.

There were more thumps from inside. Flynn's scalp crawled as he tried to decide whether there was anything he could do. He wouldn't be much good against Farooq in a fight, but he couldn't just stand here and let him beat Selim to death.

But then Farooq said, breathing hard now, "This conversation is far from over! You know what will happen, do you not, if I find out that Holmes is still alive? You know what I will do to you—and to your sister?"

There was another second's worth of silence. Flynn pictured Selim on the floor, now, doubled over from all the blows Farooq had landed. Then he said, "I know."

"Ma'a as-salaama, then," Farooq said.

Flynn barely had time to jump aside and plaster himself against the wall before the door flew the rest of the way open and Farooq came out.

Luckily he wasn't worrying about looking around, and the darkness and the fog hid Flynn enough that Farooq never spotted him, just strode off down the alley towards the lights of the gin palace.

Flynn waited another minute or so, then stepped in through the open door. "Selim Todros?"

Selim was just dragging himself painfully up off the bare wooden floorboards of the meeting room. At the sound of

Flynn's voice, he jumped and gave a half-strangled yell, clapping his hand to his heart. "Ya lahwy!" His eyes were so wide they were half starting out of his head as he stared at Flynn. "Who are you? How do you know my name?"

"Keep your voice down!" Flynn told him. "I'm from Mr. Holmes."

"Mr. Holmes?" Selim kept on staring, wiping blood away from his mouth. He'd got a split lip and one of his eyes was swelling shut. "But you are nothing but a boy—a child."

Flynn bristled. He heard plenty of that from the rest of the world, but he didn't need to take it from a man who'd just got himself used as a human punching bag.

"That's why I'm useful to Mr. Holmes. I can follow people, keep a watch on them, and no one notices I'm there. No one pays any mind to just another kid on the streets."

Selim got to his feet, wincing. "There is something in what you say," he said cautiously. "But why have you come here tonight? Unless—" a flash of anxiety crossed his eyes. "Has Mr. Holmes sent word from Egypt? Is there news about Safiya?"

"Nothing like that. I came here tonight to talk to you—and I came inside because it sounded like you could use a hand."

"Thank you, but I am quite well. I do not need any help." He stopped and sucked in a quick breath as he tried to take a step.

Flynn shook his head. "Yeah, no one's buying that bridge, mate."

"Bridge?" Selim gave him a blank look. "What bridge?"

"I heard everything Farooq just said to you," Flynn said patiently.

Flynn didn't think Farooq actually knew for a fact that Selim was lying about Mr. Holmes's death. He suspected, maybe, but he'd mostly made the accusation as an excuse for hitting Selim, just because he liked hitting people. Flynn knew Farooq's type.

"Why were the two of you speaking English, anyway?" he asked Selim. It hadn't occurred to him until now that he shouldn't have been able to understand everything that Farooq and Selim said.

"Farooq insists on it for the meetings." Selim dug out a handkerchief and pressed it against his bleeding lip. "He says that we must practise our English, the better to be prepared when the time comes for us to present our demands to the men who govern Britain. That is what he has always said," Selim added. "But lately—lately I have begun to think that it is not the only reason. Mr. Holmes was certain that Farooq is not Egyptian, but Turkish. Perhaps he is afraid that his accent will give him away if he speaks to us in Arabic too often."

"Either way, you're going to be in trouble if Farooq finds out that he's right, and Mr. Holmes isn't really dead," Flynn said.

"I know." Apparently Selim had decided that talking to a kid about his troubles was better than nothing, because his shoulders slumped and he said, "But what can I do? Mr. Holmes is not dead. How can I hope to prove otherwise?"

"You can't," Flynn said. "Unless you can get hold of a dead body that looks exactly like Mr. Holmes, the best thing to do is find out what Farooq's up to and get him locked up for it before he can hurt you or Mr. Holmes or anyone else."

They'd have to go slowly and carefully. If word got back to Lord Sonnebourne that Farooq had been arrested and the weapons seized, he might hurt Miss Zoe or Safiya. But he and Selim could start the investigation, so that everything would be in place if Mr. Holmes managed to track down Sonnebourne.

When, Flynn corrected himself. Mr. Holmes wasn't going to let a madman like Lord Sonnebourne win.

"We'd better get out of here before one of Farooq's lot comes back," Flynn said. "Any idea what Farooq meant when he said he'd got something better than the guns and ammunition?"

"No." Selim looked like he was about to be sick, although that might have been just from being punched in the stomach. "I do not know—I cannot imagine. But he is planning something. At the meeting tonight, he spoke of how the streets of London would soon run red with blood."

Now Flynn was the one who felt sick, but he said, "Then we'd better find Farooq's hiding spot."

"But where? It might be anywhere!"

"Not quite." An idea had begun to take shape in his mind, though. Hazy as the fog outside, but getting clearer the more he thought. "I've got an idea about where we can start looking."

CHAPTER 10: LUCY

Cairo was even more enchantingly picturesque than the guide-books claimed. Everywhere I looked, every corner Watson and I turned seemed to lead to a scene that might have been straight out of a painting.

The houses were high and narrow, with windows of delicate turned latticework in old brown wood. Here and there were buildings with walls faced in old carved stone. The streets themselves were roofed in overhead with long rafters and pieces of matting to provide shade from the fierce noonday sun.

Dusty sunbeams struggled through here and there, casting patches of shadow upon the moving crowd, which was an even more dizzying mix of nationalities than a London street scene. There were barefoot Egyptian peasants, wearing ragged blue shirts and felt skull-caps, Greeks in stiff white tunics, Bedouins in flowing white robes and head-scarfs, and women of the poorer class in black veils that left only their eyes uncovered.

Mixed in among them were English and other Europeans in palm-leaf hats and knickerbockers, riding depressed looking donkeys so tiny that the riders' legs almost touched the ground.

We passed by a Turkish vendor selling lemonade from a tin jar, an itinerant slipper-vendor with bright-coloured shoes dangling at the end of his long pole, and a train of supercilious-looking camels, laden with canvas-wrapped bundles.

And I couldn't enjoy any of it.

I kept scanning the faces of every long-haired dervish we passed, and studying the movements of every porter who stopped to refill his goatskin bag with water from one of the tiled public fountains.

Holmes had assumed more outlandish disguises than those in the past. Every time a seller of bead necklaces or cheap scarabs approached us to offer his wares—although insistently wave them in our faces would have been a more accurate description—I found myself wondering whether one of them would prove to be Sherlock Holmes.

Keeping a watch for him at least served to distract me from thinking about Jack and Becky, back in London. Or partly distract me.

Our discovery of Paul Archer's presence here in Cairo was a graphic reminder of just how extensively Sonnebourne's web of intrigue reached. And if he found it amusing to involve a man who had simply been one of Watson's old school friends, he would be even more motivated to endanger—

Watson's thoughts appeared to be running along the same lines as mine, because he interrupted my unpleasant reverie to say, "Becky would have loved to have seen all of this."

He was watching an Egyptian lady who was passing by. She rode a large grey donkey led by a servant in a red turban with a gleaming sabre thrust through the sash of his robe.

The lady wore a rose-coloured silk dress and white veil, and purple velvet slippers. Her arms were jangling with massive gold bracelets.

"Yes, she would."

Jack hadn't been able to leave Scotland Yard to come along, and Becky had consented to stay in London with far less argument than I would have expected.

But now I wished overwhelmingly that both of them could be here, just so that I would know that they were safe. If anything happened to them, it might be days before word reached us here—

I trampled on that thought.

The donkey and rider passed us by. The animal was just as elaborately dressed as his rider, his legs and hindquarters painted in yellow and blue and white zigzags. His saddle was covered with velvet embroidered in silver and gold thread, and his headgear was decorated with gold tassels and fringes.

"Perhaps it's lucky that Becky isn't here to see," Watson said. "She would probably be inspired to outfit Prince with a similar rig."

"Probably." I glanced up at him. "Are you certain that you wish to confront Dr. Olfrig personally?"

"I am certain of two things." Watson's voice hardened as he spoke. "First, that his purpose here in Cairo is unlikely to be innocent, and second, that I have a score to settle with him."

We had passed by bazaars selling slippers and carpets, and were entering the Khan Khaleel. The alleys were so narrow that Watson and I could scarcely walk side by side. He had to draw ahead a little and say, over his shoulder,

"And yes, I am fully aware that Holmes would not want me to let my resentment of Olfrig interfere with the case."

"He would very likely say that, yes."

In this case, though, I wasn't entirely sure that my father would be correct.

Holmes might disdain them, but anger and the desire to protect loved ones were both powerful motivators. At the moment, thinking about Jack and Becky back at home—and my mother, a prisoner—I felt fully capable of dragging Lord Sonnebourne off to prison myself, if only I'd known where to find him.

"I only meant that we ought to formulate some sort of plan," I said. "So that we can best induce Dr. Olfrig to give us as much information about Sonnebourne as possible."

Watson opened his mouth to reply, then stopped.

The shops that lined the street were tiny, barely more than cupboards with tiers of little drawers and pigeon-holes. Customers sat on stone benches in front of the cupboards, while the merchants squatted, cross-legged, inside, and took out gold and silver ornaments from the drawers: chains and earrings, anklets, bangles, necklaces strung with coins or tusk-shaped pendants.

The bench in front of the shop nearest to us was occupied by a man in European dress, and I saw at once what had given Watson pause: tall and thin, the man wore a solar topee that shaded his face and the back of his neck, and a grey houndstooth suit that I recognised immediately as one of Holmes's.

"I say, Holmes—" Watson began, striding forward.

The man turned and glanced up incuriously at our approach, revealing an ebony-black face, lined with age, rheumy dark eyes, and a nearly toothless mouth.

Watson stopped short, and I stared.

"He's definitely not—" I began.

A ragged beggar with matted grey hair and an equally matted beard that reached nearly to his waist shuffled up and took hold of Watson's sleeve.

"*Baksheesh*, kind sir? Spare a coin for a poor old—"

"Not now!" Watson tried to shake the man off, but the beggar only clung more tightly, lowering his voice.

"Come, Watson, not a word of greeting for your old friend?"

Watson's jaw dropped open, and even though I had been expecting something of the kind, I couldn't help but stare.

"I judged it expedient to hire a decoy, just in case anyone else observed my message in the hotel registry and tried to attend today's meeting," Holmes said.

He extracted a handful of coins from an inner pocket of his tattered cotton robe and dropped them into the decoy Holmes's palm. He spoke a few words in Arabic to the elderly man, who bobbed his head, smiled, and then shuffled off with a reply in Arabic—probably a word of thanks for the new suit of clothes.

"Come," Holmes said. "There is a convenient coffee house on the next street over, where we can speak in private and you can bring me up to date on what has occurred."

CHAPTER 11: FLYNN

The house where Doctor Watson had been held prisoner was in Lavender Hill, just across from Clapham Common.

The house itself was clean and respectable enough from the outside. You'd never guess from the look of the place that a villain like Lord Sonnebourne owned it and used it for kidnapping and all sorts of other dirty business.

Beside him, Selim was eyeing the house, too.

This was a busy road, with carriages and wagons rolling past all the time, women shoppers out with baskets over their arms, and street vendors selling bunches of Christmas holly and mistletoe.

"The house looks deserted," Selim murmured. "And surely the police have searched it before this?"

"Course they did. That's why we're here." Flynn spoke with more confidence than he actually felt, hoping his theory was right. "Sonnebourne's got a few places outside of London, and probably more than a couple inside the city, too. But Mr. Holmes—or Mr. Mycroft—have found them all and gone through them by now. Sonnebourne's off in Egypt, now. He doesn't have time to be buying new houses and helping his people set up shop in them. More likely he'd want to go back to a deserted place—someplace the police have already looked, and where he can be certain they wouldn't look again."

"I suppose." Selim didn't look as if he was convinced. "So what do we do?"

"We have a look around, of course." Flynn was starting to wonder what exactly Selim had learned at his fancy university classes. "Quietly, though."

The lock on the shutters that covered the window at the back of the house was an unusually tricky one; it took Flynn a couple of minutes of fiddling before he got it open. Selim, though, looked impressed.

"How did you learn to do that?"

"Practice," Flynn said. "Now get inside before someone sees us."

He'd picked out a window that was all the way around the other side of the house from the side that faced on the grey-haired neighbour's property. But it was still even odds that someone—maybe even a copper—would walk by and spot them.

Selim ducked through the window, caught his heel on the sash, and went sprawling into the room. Flynn shook his head. If they both got through this operation without being arrested or worse, it was going to be a miracle.

Although on the other hand, they could be pretty certain the house was empty. The amount of noise Selim had just made falling on his face would have brought anyone inside the place running to see what the ruckus was.

Flynn scrambled over the sill, dropped to the floor, and pulled the window down behind him, pulling the curtains shut for good measure. The room was dim, but he could see they were in a small, narrow room. There were shelves along one wall filled with all sorts of bottles, but the only furniture was a kind of medical exam table—the kind Flynn and Selim had just slept on last night in Dr. Watson's surgery—and a straight-backed wooden chair. The walls were bare white, except for a heavy portrait of an old man in a black suit and a neck-ruff, who was glaring out of the picture as if he'd been plotting to murder whoever was doing the painting.

Flynn's heart sped up. He'd heard Dr. Watson talk about that portrait. He walked up, ran his fingers across the paint, then put his eye up to the spy hole he'd just found. He could see into the next room, just like Dr. Watson had said.

Selim asked, "What is it?"

"Not sure."

The room next door wasn't just an office anymore, the way it had been when Dr. Watson was held prisoner. There was a chemical apparatus set up on the desk—beakers and test tubes and a gas ring burner, the same as Mr. Holmes had in Baker Street.

"We need to go have a look at whatever's in there, though," Flynn said.

Somehow he didn't think Farooq was just practicing chemical experiments from textbooks, the way Mr. Holmes did.

A painted black door led into the next room. Flynn stopped for a moment, listening, before heading over to the desk, but the house was still quiet.

"Potassium nitrate." He read the label off of a small box. The box was empty, but there was a dusting of white powder inside. Flynn set it down, then turned to an empty bottle that also stood on the desk. "And sul—sulfuric acid? I don't know what either of those do."

"I do." Selim looked like someone had just punched him in the stomach all over again. "I had a chemistry class last term at university. Potassium nitrate and sulfuric acid are the ingredients for making nitroglycerin, which is a highly powerful explosive. Farooq is manufacturing a bomb."

For a second, Flynn's breath went out like he'd just been struck, too. Then he pulled himself together and started to look around the room.

"What are you doing?" Selim's voice sounded scared. "We need to get out of here. If Farooq comes back—"

"Then we'll hear him coming and find someplace to hide—or get out through the window," Flynn said. "But look—there's no more potassium nitrate or sulfuric acid here, it's all been used up. So where's this nitro-glycerin stuff? If it's here, we need to find it. What are we looking for, a liquid?"

"Yes. It is colourless, slightly oily." Selim's throat contracted as he swallowed. "But if you see anything of that kind, do not touch it, nitroglycerin is highly unstable. Even the slightest jolt can cause it to detonate."

Flynn's pulse skipped. This just got better and better. "No touching. Right."

Working together, they went over the whole house, but they didn't find any bottles or anything else the nitroglycerin could have been stored in.

At last Flynn straightened from where he'd been looking under the cast-iron stove in the kitchen and said, "The stuff's not here."

Selim tried to take a breath but turned green and clutched his middle. He'd probably got a couple of bruised ribs. Flynn knew from experience how much those hurt.

"What do we do now?"

"Get you some place where you can rest, for one thing."

"Not Baker Street!" Selim looked scared. "I do not know for certain, but I think Farooq is having the place watched in case Mr. Holmes returns there."

Flynn snorted. "As if Mr. Holmes would be that much of a mug. And no, we're going to go to see a friend of mine."

Becky had just barely agreed to let him come out tonight without her, since she'd grudgingly admitted that the two of them would stand out more than just Flynn on his own. But she'd still be awake, waiting to hear his report when he came back as he'd promised.

"Her brother's a copper. We can tell him what we found here, and he'll get the police searching for places where Farooq might have planted the bomb."

Selim looked like he was hesitating, but finally he said, "All right. I will come."

CHAPTER 12: WATSON

Holmes seemed to know the proprietor of the coffee shop, who escorted us to a back room concealed from the front of the establishment by a hanging beaded curtain. There, over tiny cups of a steaming dark brew, we gave Holmes an account of our meeting with Paul Archer.

Holmes listened in silence, his eyes half-lidded, and when we had finished, leaned back in his chair.

"So Dr. Olfrig is in Cairo."

"Yes. His presence is unlikely to be for any innocent reason," Watson said.

"Indeed. Especially when coupled with the fact that the German Foreign Minister is present in the city, as well."

"Von Bulow is here?" I asked sharply.

"Suggestive, is it not?" Holmes paused. "And you are to meet with Dr. Olfrig at the Cairo Museum this afternoon."

"Unless you would have us do otherwise."

"Not at all." Holmes's posture was still languid, but I detected a familiar gleam in his grey eyes. "I think a meeting with Dr. Olfrig—provided the conditions are right—could prove most instructive."

"But you do not wish to accompany us?" Lucy asked.

"For the moment, I prefer to remain deceased in the eyes of the world, although I strongly suspect that the ruse will not have fooled Sonnebourne. Farooq may have been gulled with relative ease, but a man of Lord Sonnebourne's intelligence must surely have doubts that our accident in London was genuine. However, he cannot be certain, nor is he aware of my exact location, and I would prefer that it remain so."

Holmes considered a moment, then extracted a pencil and paper from his beggar's robe and wrote a few lines on it. "This is the name of a man who may be of help to you when you arrive at the museum. He has recently been appointed Inspector of Monuments for Upper Egypt in the Egyptian Antiquities Service, and as such makes his residence in Luxor. But he is visiting Cairo for the Christmas season. He is also an old acquaintance of mine. Ask for him, and give him the note I have written. I believe he will be willing to assist in your plans."

* * *

Sometime later, Lucy and I were mounting the steps to the Cairo Museum. Once home to a large hareem for hundreds of young Egyptian women, the palace now housed selected Egyptian artifacts, on a temporary basis, while a new and improved edifice for the main Cairo museum was being constructed.

"What is the name of the man Holmes told us to contact?" Lucy asked.

I took the folded paper Holmes had given me from my pocket and read aloud. "Howard Carter. I confess that I've never heard of him. And I've no idea how Holmes knows him."

"I suppose neither of us should be surprised that Holmes has helpful acquaintances even here, in Egypt," Lucy said.

Archer met us inside the doors. "Watson, delighted to see you again. Come with me, Dr. Olfrig was delighted to hear that you were in Cairo and looks forward to meeting you again."

"Does he indeed." I took firmer hold of my temper. "Thank you for arranging the meeting."

"He's waiting for us in one of the display rooms," Archer went on. "There's a fundraiser going on—one of his fellow countrymen, a German archaeologist is putting on an … ah, demonstration. Of a kind." Archer seemed a trifle nervous, and he cast a dubious glance at Lucy. "I'm afraid, though, that you may find it rather, ah, unpleasant."

"Perhaps. But I imagine that I've seen worse," Lucy said. She smiled at Archer, though, to take away the sting of the words and said, "Lead the way, Mr. Archer, we're quite ready."

The display room was crowded with people, all of whom were ogling a bespectacled old German doctor who had set himself up on a dais at the head of the room.

He stood beside a mummy, its torso and head affixed to a hand-cranked axle, and was turning it as though it were a roast on a spit.

The mummy spun slowly, unwinding the strips of gauze that formed its wrappings. The lower extremities had been the first to come free, and they flopped, stiff and awkward, the joints making creaking and cracking noises as the tendons and sinews ruptured.

The dead tissue that had once been a living woman of high birth now resembled a grotesque clown attempting to rouse itself.

"See how our noble lady dances for us!" said the German.

"Not too rapidly, of course, for that would damage the connective tissue."

Beside me, Archer's face was pinched with distaste, but he threaded a way through the crowd, approaching a man the sight of whom made my blood run cold.

Dr. Clovis Olfrig straightened and turned at our arrival. Small and grey-haired, his eyes glittered behind wire-rimmed spectacles.

"Doctor Watson!" He stretched out a hand. "It is a pleasure to see you again."

I felt my temper rising again. I wondered if this was some residual effect of the drug he had used three years ago to interview me. More likely, I thought, it was the result of seeing him for the first time after those three years. Being face to face with him could very well have triggered a great deal of hitherto-suppressed but highly justified resentment.

But whatever the cause, I had the sudden urge to strike the man.

"Likewise," I told him.

"I'm sorry." Lucy put her hand up to her forehead. "It must be the heat—or the—" she gestured to the mummy, now bared up to the tops of the legs. "I feel quite faint. Mr. Archer, would you mind …"

Paul, ever gallant, sprang to offer her his arm and to escort her from the room.

Olfrig watched them go, his expression benevolent. "Ah, it is perhaps not a sight for the delicate sensibilities of the fairer sex. But an excellent means of procuring funds to further our excavations here in Egypt. You would be surprised at what your countrymen will pay to witness the desecration of an ancient noblewoman's remains."

I ignored the implied insult. "The German government is interested in archaeological research?" I asked.

"The Kaiser is interested in all sciences that advance mankind's knowledge!"

And the presence of German teams of excavators here in Egypt, I thought, offered an excellent source of cover for spying on the British troops stationed here and at the nearby Suez Canal.

But I refrained from saying as much out loud.

"Perhaps there is somewhere we might converse privately?" I asked.

Behind the lenses of his spectacles, Olfrig's gaze was as hard and as speculative as that of a serpent. But he nodded. "By all means, Dr. Watson, by all means. The office of Herr von Bork"— he indicated the man in charge of unwrapping the mummy— "will be empty; we can go there."

The office door was part way open. The little room was cluttered with broken bits of pottery and small stone statuary in the ancient Egyptian style. Shelves, a desk, and two visitor's chairs were the only furniture.

"Now, Dr. Watson," Olfrig said, seating himself behind the desk. "My condolences to you upon your loss of Mr. Holmes. I read about it in the papers."

"A most unfortunate accident," I said.

"And did you certify the death?" asked Olfrig. "As a man of science, I would have thought—"

I felt my emotions rise once again. But since that was precisely the response he was hoping to provoke in me, I allowed my anger to show this time. "Not appropriate," I said. "Your question, I mean, is not appropriate. I will not discuss it."

But the little grey-haired doctor was not to be put off so readily.

"Of course, it would have been an emotional event for you to witness," he said, "with you being his friend and close associate. I am merely curious as to whether you were able to put aside your natural feelings—"

"I am not here to gratify your curiosity," I said.

"Ah." Olfrig leaned back in his chair.

With the mummy unwrapping still going on downstairs, this area of the museum was entirely quiet, although I had failed to completely shut the door. Now I heard the sound of footsteps in the hall outside the office we were borrowing, but whoever it was passed by without coming in.

Olfrig put the tips of his fingers together. "That begs the question of why you are here? I should have thought that your memories of the time you spent in my care at my clinic in Bad Homburg would have, shall we say, deterred you from seeking out another meeting?"

I wanted to seize Olfrig by the lapels and haul him from his chair. I wanted to shatter that smug, officious confidence and turn it into fear.

But I said, evenly, "I met with Paul Archer at Shepheard's Hotel this morning. He told me of your hopes for the antivenin venture."

"And you wished to warn him against working with me?" Olfrig asked. "Or perhaps—now, here is a thought—you wish to offer your own services as a physician, so that you may share in the profits? After all, with Mr. Holmes dead, you will have double your rent in Baker Street to pay."

"You are deliberately trying to provoke me," I said.

Olfrig's face creased in a smile.

"Unfortunately for you," I went on, "you have been so busy

in attempting to goad me into losing my temper that you have neglected to notice that you are alone here with me. Or that my traveling companion has just joined us and is currently aiming a pistol directly at you from her vantage point outside in the hall."

Lucy, having alerted me to her presence by walking past the office, had returned more silently and now pushed the door fully open. As I had stated, she had drawn her Ladysmith pistol and was aiming it directly at Dr. Olfrig's heart.

I would not have been human if I had not felt satisfaction at the way the color ebbed from the doctor's face, leaving it a sickly, mottled gray.

His hand made a jerky movement towards the pocket of his jacket, where I surmised he very likely had a weapon of his own.

"Oh, please do try it." Lucy flicked the safety catch off her gun. "I will be delighted if you give me a reason to shoot you."

Olfrig's face blanched further and he moistened his lips with the tip of his tongue. "What is the meaning of this?"

"We want to know about Lord Sonnebourne," I told him. "Why he is in Egypt, and where he is now."

"I don't know what you mean! I am here to conduct scientific research—"

"Spare me your lies," I snapped. "You gave yourself away when you tried to provoke me by commiserating on Holmes's death, which you had seen reported in the newspapers. There have been no such reports."

The two days Lucy and I had spent in our required quarantine period upon arriving in Alexandria had given me ample opportunity of perusing the papers, looking for stories of Holmes's death. There were none. Nor were there references to the Sons of Ra. The British papers seemed preoccupied with the growing unrest in South Africa, and the call in Parliament for a vast increase in the number of troops to be sent there to quell the Boers.

The Egyptian papers—those which were printed in English—featured news of the dam across the Nile at Aswan, now under construction by a British engineering firm. I recalled that Holmes had focused on similar stories when we had been in London.

The stories I read in the Egyptian papers focused on considerable debate over the project, due to the projected flooding of an ancient temple no longer in active use. Those opposed to the dam wished to preserve a valuable historic artifact. Those in favour trumpeted that the financial terms to Egypt were wonderfully generous, and that no payments to the British firm would be made unless the dam was completed and profitable.

"You are a known associate of Herr Von Bulow, who is also in Cairo," I went on. "And since we also know that Sonnebourne is in the pay of the Kaiser—and moreover is the only man in Egypt who would have had word of Holmes death—I repeat: where is Sonnebourne and what are his plans?"

Dr. Olfrig swallowed but once again attempted to bluster. "I do not have to sit here and listen to your threats and your insults—"

"Actually, yes, you do," Lucy said. "Unless you would prefer that I shoot you."

"You would commit murder?" Olfrig's upper lip curled.

"Oh, I wouldn't kill you," Lucy said calmly. "Only shoot you in the arm or the knee or somewhere equally painful but non-fatal. You would of course be welcome to file a complaint with the Egyptian police."

The police force in Egypt, like nearly every other branch of the government, was ultimately controlled by the British. I saw in Olfrig's expression how little he liked the idea of attracting their notice for any reason.

He swallowed again. "I … I do not know the man of whom you speak personally. However, I can tell you that a gentleman did call upon Herr Von Bulow for a meeting a few days ago, and spoke with him in private for some time."

"What did they talk of?"

"I do not know!" Olfrig's voice rose. "Their meeting was private, as I said!"

"Not good enough." Lucy advanced a step or two, the gun still trained on the doctor's mid-section and her green eyes hard. "Let us be crystal clear, Dr. Olfrig. Lord Sonnebourne has repeatedly threatened my family and has now kidnapped my mother. I am extremely short on patience with anyone who tries to hamper our catching up with him. Now, I find it very unlikely that a miserable, sneaking little worm such as yourself wouldn't have found a way to listen at the door or through a keyhole. So what did Von Bulow and Sonnebourne talk of!"

Dr. Olfrig was rattled enough that he didn't even protest at Lucy's insults, only passed his tongue once more over his dry lips. "I heard very little," he said. "Sonnebourne said something about hiring a boat—a *dahabeeyah*—for the journey to Aswan."

My heart sank. "Aswan?" Hearing that Sonnebourne was travelling to the critically important construction project, I feared we were already too late to interfere with his plans. The city was in the far south of Egypt, a journey of at least three days up the Nile. "He is no longer in Cairo, then?"

"As far as I know, he planned to leave at once. He asked Von

Bulow for money—for expenses, he said."

"Expenses? What for?" I asked.

"He did not say. Only that he hoped to give the Kaiser, the All-highest, a suitable Christmas present." Olfrig wiped a drop of perspiration from his brow, and added, "He said that it would be delivered on the 24th."

CHAPTER 13: LUCY

The waters of the Nile flowed slowly beneath us, providing little opposition to the side paddle steamer we had boarded. On either side of the great river, dun-coloured buildings shone in the sunlight, evidence that we were still well within the city of Cairo. Our choice of travelling by steamer had been quite deliberate, for we were going to the British ambassador's residence and we wished to avoid the main entrance utilised by visitors arriving in the ordinary way using carriages.

Instead, we had taken the Cook's steamer, and I could see the docking area at the rear of the building, where the great green lawn spread out beyond the bright new white stone colonnades, leading to equally bright new stone steps approaching the garden entrance.

The building itself was equally grand, newly built in the classic Grecian style and spreading out as if luxuriating in the riverfront space.

"Seems more appropriate for a king's palace," Watson said, as we stood at the steamboat railing.

It was the third member of our party who answered, a dark-haired young man in his middle twenties, with a long, intelligent face.

"An investment," Howard Carter said. "There was considerable debate in Parliament about the funding, but it was finally decided that the residence would demonstrate to the Egyptians the British commitment over the long term." He gave a wry smile. "Or, to put it another way, awe them into submission with an intimidating show of our resources and power. Like the Sphinx. Or the Tower of London, for that matter."

"Thank you for arranging this meeting for us, Mr. Carter," I said. "And for summoning the police officers to the museum."

"Only too pleased to help," Carter smiled. "Happy to hear from Holmes as well. I think he may be right about the Germans making mischief in Egypt. And this Olfrig is known to be one of the Kaiser's minions. A prize specimen, in fact."

After leaving the display room, I had found Mr. Carter and presented him with Holmes's note and request for assistance, with the result that Dr. Olfrig had been driven away in a carriage owned by the Cairo city police. Olfrig would eventually reach the British ambassador's residence for questioning by various high officials. Though I doubted they would learn more from him than we had done.

Howard Carter looked grave as he continued, "And if Olfrig is connected to this Sonnebourne fellow, then both of them must certainly be stopped. Heaven knows what deviltry they could be stirring up."

Aswan. I thought.

I pictured the newspapers piled in Holmes's sitting room. I recalled Olfrig's confession that Sonnebourne was now on his way to the location of the hugely important British construction project.

"We shall do our utmost to stop them," Watson said.

"Though of course we have no legal authority or standing here in Egypt," I added. I did not want to suggest anything specific to Carter. Better to deal with the officials responsible, such as Lord Cromer, the British Ambassador, whom we expected to meet in a few minutes' time.

Carter's sober face relaxed in a quick smile. "I wish that I had been able to see Mr. Holmes in person. He worked as a copyist on a dig several years ago, you know."

I hadn't known, nor, to judge by the slight widening of his eyes, had Watson. But neither of us expressed disbelief that Holmes should have added archaeology to the list of his many interests. As Watson had so famously said, it was impossible to delineate Sherlock Holmes's limits.

"When I was excavating in the Valley of the Kings," Carter went on. "There are those who say that the Valley is played out, that all the royal tombs have already been discovered. But Mr. Holmes was certain—and I agree with him—that the place still has secrets left to yield. He encouraged me to keep digging in the Valley, and I intend to, funds permitting. Who knows?" Carter smiled again. "Perhaps I shall discover that rarity which is every archaeologist's fondest dream, an unrobbed tomb."

* * *

We bid Mr. Carter goodbye at the boat dock and mounted through the garden and up the stone steps of the residence. A uniformed British officer stood at the gate of the colonnade, apparently deep in conversation with a man in the snowy white robe and the white headdress, or *keffiyeh*, of a wealthy Arabian.

The robed man turned at our approach, revealing Holmes's familiar features, though his skin was darkened to a medium bronze and the fierceness of his thick black brows owed more to art than to nature.

Watson drew up sharply, then let out an explosive breath.

"One day, Holmes, I will cease to be surprised when you pop up like the demon in a pantomime play."

Holmes's expression remained grave. Now that the matted hair and beard of his earlier disguise were gone, I could see he looked no more rested than he had done in London. His features were even sharper than usual, and lines of strain bracketed the corners of his mouth.

"At least one more meeting was necessary," he said. "So that I may learn of your encounter with Dr. Olfrig. I also wish to send Mycroft a telegram via more secure channels than the ordinary ones, for which I shall need to enlist Ambassador Cromer's help."

"A telegram to Mycroft?" Watson repeated.

"Yes. Paul Archer's appearance in Cairo is suggestive, is it not?"

Watson frowned. "We discussed that already. Do you mean that you intend to warn Mycroft of the potential danger on his end?"

Holmes waved a dismissive hand. "Mycroft is as aware of the danger as I am, and will be taking all due precautions." He glanced at me. "As will Jack and Becky."

"Of course." That knowledge didn't lessen the cold anxiety under my ribcage, though. But I wrenched my thoughts away from what could be happening in London. I had to trust Jack—and Becky, for that matter—to stay alive. And I had to find Lord Sonnebourne and save my mother.

"You mean," I said, "that Paul Archer's presence begs the question of exactly *how* Sonnebourne learned of our connection to him. Archer's case was never made public knowledge."

One of the two villains of our adventure with Paul at the London Zoo had been April Norman, an apparently charming and pretty young girl. She was the sort who inevitably arouse the sympathy of both judge and jury, and as such, she had been convicted for embezzlement only, not murder.

"Precisely," Holmes said. "However, let us go in. Lord Cromer awaits."

He spoke to the guard, who consulted his notebook and nodded, then beckoned us to the tall steps.

At his signal, one of the great double doors swung open to reveal the presence of another uniformed guard.

Behind him stood a somewhat portly gentleman, impeccably dressed, fresh-faced, sleek-haired and clean shaven but for a perfectly trimmed small dark moustache.

"I am Lord Cromer," he said with a bow. "Welcome to the consulate, Mr. Holmes."

"Or the Lord's House, as I believe it is called," said Holmes, stepping in and extending his hand in greeting.

Lord Cromer ushered us into a gold-trimmed conference room.

"I received your message about Dr. Olfrig, Mr. Holmes, and of course your reputation is such that he will be detained and interrogated. However, I must tell you that I am placed in somewhat of an awkward position. Already Herr Von Bulow of the German embassy has telephoned, demanding Dr. Olfrig's release."

"That was quick work." Holmes sounded entirely calm. "You can stall him?"

"Oh yes." A faint smile traced Lord Cromer's mouth. "If

there is one skill at which we diplomats excel, it is the art of prevarication and playing for time. However, since Dr. Olfrig has committed no provable crime, we will have to release him, eventually."

"That is to be expected, and matters little. Olfrig spoke of whatever Von Bulow and Lord Sonnebourne are planning coming to fruition on the 24th."

Concern stamped Lord Cromer's face. "That is only three days from now."

Holmes's expression didn't alter. "At which point, we shall either have succeeded or failed."

"Is there any way I can be of assistance?" Lord Cromer asked.

"Lucy and Dr. Watson shall proceed upriver for a journey of about three days, to Aswan, since that was the location mentioned by Olfrig. We shall want your support and protection, Lord Cromer."

"You shall have it."

I was watching Holmes closely. "But you do not intend to accompany us?"

"If all goes well, I shall hope to join you there," Holmes said. "Now, Lord Cromer, I take it there is a British garrison nearby to Aswan?"

"I'll have a word with Lord Kitchener," the ambassador said. "Military commander of the region. Just been made a baronet for his victory at Omdurman, in the Sudan, not far from Aswan."

"I read about that," Watson said. "As I recall, the enemy's losses were horrific."

"Yes, nearly forty thousand killed or wounded," the ambassador said. "Kitchener remarked afterward that war is not a time for mercy."

CHAPTER 14: FLYNN

A uniformed police constable was standing on the step of the house where Becky lived with Lucy and Jack.

He gave Flynn and Selim a hard stare as they came up, and looked like he was going to start in with the, *What's all this, then*.

But Becky's head popped out of the upstairs window.

"It's all right, Constable Polk. You can let them in."

Becky opened the door to them, and led the way into the kitchen. "Jack was called away to a murder case in Kensington, and he didn't want to take any chances, so he left Constable Polk on guard," she said. "He's nice enough. Even if he won't let me go anywhere or do anything."

Selim was looking more sickly than ever and more collapsed onto a chair than sat down.

"Does he need a doctor, do you think?" Becky asked.

"No." Selim had closed his eyes, but shook his head and drew a breath. "No, I need no doctor."

Becky was eyeing him the way Mr. Holmes looked at a specimen under a microscope. "If he's got bruised or cracked ribs, there's not very much a doctor could do, anyway. I read about it in one of Dr. Watson's medical textbooks." She looked at Flynn. "All right. Tell me what's been happening."

Flynn brought her up to date on the night's events. Becky listened, her eyes widening a bit when he got to the part about the nitroglycerin.

"We'd better send word to Scotland Yard. I'll tell Constable Polk so that he can come in and use the telephone; they'll be more likely to listen to him than to me."

She went out of the kitchen, and a few moments later, Flynn heard the police constable telephoning from the next room.

Becky was frowning when she came back into the room.

"There's something that doesn't make sense," she said.

"About the bomb Farooq's planning?" Flynn asked.

"No. It's about Safiya."

Flynn had thought Selim had fallen asleep, he was leaning back in his chair with his eyes shut again. But at that he started up.

"What about Safiya?"

Selim's voice went tight and his face looked strained every time his sister's name came up.

Flynn felt sorry for him, but not sorry enough to keep quiet. This might be important, and he thought he knew what was in Becky's mind.

"Becky's right, she's just an ordinary Egyptian girl. I know she's your sister, but there's nothing all that special about her."

"Flynn!" Becky said.

It had sounded less rude in his head than when he'd said it out loud. "Sorry. What I mean is, why would Sonnebourne bother carting her with him all the way to Egypt?"

Becky nodded. "Exactly. If he's trying to blackmail you into killing Mr. Holmes by keeping her hostage, he could just as easily have found someplace here in England to keep her. It doesn't make sense he'd pay for her passage to Egypt. Even for a man as rich as Sonnebourne, that can't have been cheap."

If anything, Selim looked even more worried than he had a minute ago, with his mouth set tight and his hands clenched into fists in his lap.

But he said, after swallowing, "I do not know. I cannot explain it."

"There's something else," Flynn said.

He'd been given the assignment to keep an eye on the building that housed Farooq's stockpile of weapons. He was to report back to Mr. Mycroft Holmes straight away if he saw anything— like Farooq taking the weapons away to be handed out to his men, for example. But so far, nothing had happened.

By now, Flynn had got to thinking that out of all the dangerous jobs he done for Mr. Holmes, the one that looked to do him in was this one, which might kill him with sheer boredom.

But a good thing about all the hours and days he'd spent watching the weapons storehouse, was that he'd had plenty of time to think.

He'd been remembering everything he'd overheard on the night he'd first followed Farooq and listened in on Farooq speaking to one of his men.

None of the words had been in English, but Flynn had been turning what he'd overheard over and over inside his head, and he thought he could at least remember some of the sounds. More than he'd been able to recall for Mr. Holmes, when Mr. Holmes had asked.

That was why he'd sought out Selim tonight in the first place at the Sons of Ra meeting.

"I was wondering. Could you tell me what"—Flynn tried to say the word exactly as he'd heard it. "What bar-la-man means?"

He thought Selim looked a bit relieved at the change of subject. "It means parliament. Like your English government."

Flynn nodded. He supposed that didn't help too much. The weapons cache was just about next door to the Houses of Parliament—just up the river.

For all he knew, Farooq had been telling the other man that he'd know what time it was when Big Ben, the clock in the tower of the Parliament building, chimed.

"What about … urabi?" Flynn was sure he had heard Farooq say that word more than once.

Flynn wasn't even positive he'd got the pronunciation right. He definitely wasn't ready for Selim's face to go from green to grey-ish, or for him to seem ready to topple off the chair and onto the kitchen floor.

"Ur-urabi?" Selim repeated. His voice sounded like he was choking on something.

"I think so. Why, what's it mean?"

"I … I am not sure." Selim wiped his forehead with the back of his hand. "I am not familiar. But perhaps it might be someone's name?"

CHAPTER 15: ZOE

"Early supper and bed-time tonight," Mrs. Orles said.

As usual, the younger woman's voice made Zoe think of a beaker of cloyingly sweet poison.

She turned from their stateroom window, where she'd been watching the palm-fringed banks of the Nile slide past as their boat sailed upriver against the current.

Beyond the palm groves, tracts of young corn showed green on the flat banks and the occasional small whitewashed minaret reached its spire up towards a sky that was turning dusky purple with the approach of evening.

"Why?" Zoe asked.

Most of the day had been spent undergoing the arduous process of portaging, which meant that their boat had been dragged up the cataract portions of the river by brawny Nubians, using dozens of stout ropes and their own strong arms and legs to move the vessel.

Zoe had been confined to her stateroom—as she had been every day of their voyage—but the *dahabeeyah* was small enough that she had overheard the reis, or captain, of the boat tell Sonnebourne that in the rainy season these laborious services would not have been required, due to the increased depth of water in the river channel.

Fortunately, Reis Hassan had said, as they passed the small river city of Aswan, there was still enough water in the channel to support the vessel the entire two miles of alternating cataract slopes and level pools that they were about to traverse.

A short while later, Reis Hassan had pointed to a bustling construction site along the river, proudly proclaiming it to be the new dam that the British were constructing. The dam would be of huge economic import to the region, and indeed to the entire nation of Egypt itself.

Now they were approaching an island—she had overheard the crew refer to it as Philae—in the middle of the great river. The ancient stone temple structures on the crown of the island loomed above it, cast into silhouette by the twilight rays of the sun, now well below the horizon.

Mrs. Orles shook her head in answer to Zoe's question, waving her index finger as she would have done to correct a naught child. "Now, now, that's for me to know, and for you to find out. Or rather"—she gave a high-pitched and equally venomous little laugh—"*not* to find out."

Zoe was spared the temptation to murder Mrs. Orles by the entrance of the serving boy, who put a tray of food—stew and thick, round flats of bread—down on the table in front of Mrs. Orles.

"Shukraan," Zoe murmured.

The boy—a skinny Egyptian child of eleven or twelve with a head of curly dark hair—gave her a quick, frightened glance from under his long lashes.

There was a fresh bruise on his cheek, Zoe saw, the mark of

someone's fist. She didn't have to wonder about to whom the fist had belonged. Their boat—or *dayabeeyah*, as the Egyptian sailing vessels were called—had separate cabins for herself and Safiya, Mrs. Orles, and each of the men. But their quarters were closely confined enough that she could hear Mr. Morgan shouting and cursing at the boat's crew for failing to polish his shoes correctly, or bring him his preferred type of cigarettes or after-dinner whiskey, or a hundred other offenses he had found to complain of on their journey. Mr. Morgan hated everything about Egypt. He disliked the food and the native Egyptian people intensely, and had the lowest possible opinion of the sanitary measures available.

Zoe doubted he'd dared to actually strike any of the other crew members, who were full-grown men, wiry and tough-looking from manning sailboats.

This boy was the only one of them whom Morgan could hit without fearing that he would hit back.

Now the child ducked his head and hurried out, shutting the door behind him.

"You should not speak to the servants," Mrs. Orles snapped.

She still had neither forgiven nor forgotten Zoe's attempt to send a message through the serving girl in Brindisi.

Had Valentina found the message Zoe had hidden under the bed? And if she had, would she have actually sent it on, or was her telegram to Sherlock now lying crumpled up at the bottom of some rubbish heap?

Zoe had absolutely no way of knowing. She had felt often these past several days that if she could only know—even if the answer was that Sherlock had received no message from her at all—it would be better than the suspense of uncertainty.

She still wasn't even letting herself consider the possibility that Sherlock was dead and would never come to her aid. But she was also forcing herself to confront the fact that she wasn't the princess in a fairy tale, and Sherlock, even assuming that he was alive, had always been an extremely unlikely prince. As things now stood, she was on her own—and if she was going to escape, it would have to be by her own wits and ingenuity.

The trouble was that her mind kept coming up empty of any practical ideas of getting away. They had been on the river for two days, now—and for most of that time, her mind had been spinning, examining and ultimately discarding each and every plan that occurred to her as impossible.

She could—theoretically—jump off of the boat sometime in the middle of the night, when Mrs. Orles was asleep. But even if she was willing to risk Sonnebourne retaliating by harming Safiya, where would she go? She might swim to shore. She knew how to swim; that was one small point in her favor. But that would only bring her to an unfamiliar riverbank in a foreign land, where she knew no one, didn't speak the language, and where her European clothing and pale skin would stand out like a lone untuned instrument in a string quartet.

"I was only trying to be polite," she told Mrs. Orles meekly. She picked up one of the rounds of bread and took a bite, ignoring Mrs. Orles's hard stare as the housekeeper evidently tried to decide whether or not she was up to something.

Even she—or Lord Sonneborne, for that matter—would be hard pressed to see the serving boy as a likely co-conspirator. So far, Zoe hadn't managed to get him to speak a single word to her. And in any case, *shukraan*—thank you—was the sum total of Zoe's Arabic.

Finally, Mrs. Orles turned to Safiya, who was pale-faced and silent, swaying a little in her chair.

"Eat." She pushed a bowl of the unidentifiable stew towards the Egyptian girl.

Safiya looked at the bowl blankly and made no move to do as she was told. Her eyes looked both dazed and yet over-bright, and there were bright spots of color on her cheeks that made Zoe think she might be running a fever.

With an exclamation of annoyance, Mrs. Orles picked up the soup bowl and held it up to Safiya's lips. The girl made a weak motion with one hand as though trying to push it away, and turned her head.

"Drink!"

A little of the liquid slopped over the edge of the bowl and ran down Safiya's chin, but the girl didn't swallow.

"Drink it, you little fool!" Mrs. Orles's hand flashed out, delivering a ringing slap to Safiya's cheek.

Zoe clenched her fists, fighting the urge to snatch the bowl straight out of Mrs. Orles's hands and upend it over the housekeeper's head. Safiya, though, only blinked.

"Would you like me to try feeding her?" Zoe asked. She kept her tone level, silently blessing a career that had been spent dealing with temperamental orchestra conductors and sopranos who gave new meaning to the term prima donna. She had a good deal of practice at sounding calm while inwardly seething with rage.

Mrs. Orles's eyes narrowed, clearly trying to decide whether there was any chance of Zoe's somehow turning this to her advantage. During the long pause that followed, Zoe held the housekeeper's gaze, keeping her expression polite but indifferent.

After what seemed an eternity, Mrs. Orles huffed out a breath. "Very well. You may see what you can do."

She rose to her feet and went out. Zoe knew from experience that Mrs. Orles would be fetching the small brown bottle of laudanum from her own room, the one that she used for dosing Safiya each morning and night.

She would be gone for a few precious seconds.

Zoe reached out quickly, picking up the dish of clarified butter that had been provided for dipping the bread. Her pulse was beating from her eardrums all the way out to the tips of her fingers, but what she intended didn't take long.

By the time Mrs. Orles came back to the table, laudanum in hand, Zoe was innocently holding a spoon up to Safiya's lips and trying to coax her to sip a little of the broth.

Mrs. Orles still gave her a hard stare as she sat down again with a thump, reaching for Safiya's teacup so that she could pour in the measured dose of laudanum.

The cup slipped from her fingers, fell to the floor, and smashed.

Zoe had just greased the outside of it with the clarified butter.

Mrs. Orles uttered an exclamation of irritation, setting the laudanum bottle down on the table and going to the door.

"Daoud!" Her voice echoed in the narrow confines of the passageway outside their stateroom, and Zoe heard the tap of her heels retreating towards the back of the ship. "Daoud!"

Zoe snatched up the laudanum bottle. It was about half full.

She uncorked it, poured a generous amount of the murky brown fluid into the cup of coffee that sat beside Mrs. Orles's place at the table. Then she flew to the side of their stateroom, and dumped the rest of the laudanum out of the porthole into the waters of the Nile below.

In the bare handful of seconds it took, she noted that their boat appeared to have dropped anchor, and that they were within only a few yards of their destination, the temple island of Philae.

Well, that might come in useful, too.

Zoe had just time enough to refill the laudanum bottle from her own cup of tea and set it back on the table before Mrs. Orles returned, carrying a replacement teacup and muttering under her breath about the impossible nature of native servants and the revolting standards of cleanliness in this dreadful country.

She seemed to entirely share Mr. Morgan's opinion of Egypt.

The boy—Daoud—trailed behind her, looking even more frightened than usual. Zoe felt a prick of conscience for letting him in for a scolding over his carelessness in serving a dirty teacup. But her primary feeling was one of overwhelming relief.

Mrs. Orles didn't seem to suspect anything amiss.

The boy knelt to sweep up the fragments of the broken cup. Mrs. Orles, her face still flushed with irritation, tipped a measure from the laudanum bottle into the new teacup she'd brought and held it to Safiya's lips.

"Drink it!"

This time, Safiya drank obediently, downing several swallows before she turned her head away.

Daoud finished his sweeping and went out, and Mrs. Orles picked up her own cup.

Zoe held her breath while the housekeeper drank, but she finished the cup without comment. The bitterness of the coffee was apparently enough to cover the laudanum's taste.

Now all Zoe could do was wait.

CHAPTER 16: FLYNN

Flynn woke to the sensation of being jabbed in the ribcage. He opened his eyes to find Becky leaning over him, just about to poke him again.

"Are you awake?" she asked.

"I am now." Flynn sat up.

He'd gone to sleep on the downstairs sofa, while Selim took the spare bed upstairs. Now it was almost morning, to judge by the faint grey light filtering in through the windows.

"Something wrong?"

Becky was already fully dressed and wearing her outdoor coat and gloves.

"I want to go and consult Mr. Holmes's files," she said.

Flynn rubbed his eyes. "At Baker Street? What about?"

"The name you overheard Farooq use. Urabi. I think Selim was lying when he said it didn't mean anything to him."

"You've got that right." Flynn had been tempted to tell Selim that anyone who couldn't make up lies better than he did should give up trying. But Selim had been in bad enough shape that he hadn't had the heart to badger him.

Now Flynn swung his legs down from the sofa and reached for his coat. He'd already got his boots on, since he'd slept in them.

"Should we tell Constable what's-his-name we're going?"

So far as he knew, the copper was still standing guard outside the door.

"Polk," Becky said. "And that's just it, I don't want to tell him. He'll say that it's too risky to go to Baker Street and we ought to wait until Jack gets back—unless he comes with us, and in that case, he wouldn't be guarding Selim. And what if this is something important, something that Mr. Holmes and Lucy need to know?"

Flynn wasn't going to argue about that, either. He'd stayed awake for a long time last night, with two thoughts jabbing him, sharp as a couple of tie pins between the shoulder blades:

First, that Farooq wasn't just collecting all those weapons and the nitroglycerin so that he could put them up on some mantle shelf. He and the Sons of Ra were going to use them. People would die.

The second thought that had kept him awake, skin crawling, was the fact that Mr. Holmes could get himself killed all the way out in foreign parts.

"Let's go," he told Becky. "We can get out the back window where Constable Polk won't see."

CHAPTER 17: ZOE

Lying in her narrow stateroom bunk, Zoe strained to hear in the dark. The boat was moored for the night by the side of the river, and the only sound was the steady lap of the river waters against the hull, and the occasional snore from the crew members who slept out on the deck.

Mrs. Orles, yawning widely, had retired to her own stateroom about two hours ago by Zoe's estimation. She had been sluggish and stupefied enough that she hadn't even bothered to lock the cabin door when she went out as she usually did.

Zoe devoutly hoped that small piece of luck hadn't used up all of her allotted good fortune for the night.

The question now was whether Mrs. Orles was deeply asleep enough not to wake at the sound of movements from the room next door to her own.

Slowly, Zoe eased the thin cotton sheets back and sat up, wincing as the bed creaked. A shaft of moonlight coming through the portal window cast a pale, silvery glow over the stateroom.

What would Sherlock say about this scheme? She could imagine him commenting sardonically that it was deplorably spur-of-the-moment and ill planned. But then she could also picture him pointing out that it would be the height of illogic for her to let this opportunity slip by. Both responses would be in character.

She dressed quickly in the white shirtwaist and black skirt she'd worn to Mr. Morgan's home all those weeks ago in London. She hadn't any other clothes. The best she'd been able to manage was rinsing her things out in the washbasin and hanging them up to dry while she slept in her shift. Now they felt unpleasantly damp against her skin, but she pulled them on, put on her stockings, and laced up her boots.

Zoe crept to the window and looked out. Everything was still and quiet, the river sparkling in the moonlight.

At least, she argued with imaginary-Sherlock, luck appeared to be on her side. She'd seized the chance opportunity for drugging Mrs. Orles. But half an hour ago, she had heard Sonnebourne informing Reis Hassan that he and Mr. Morgan wished to visit the Philae temple by moonlight, and that he was to bring them ashore.

The Reis was a big, phlegmatic man who apparently had absorbed the British philosophy of *ours not to question why*. Zoe had watched from their stateroom window as he maneuvered round the upstream tip of the island and then let the vessel drift back, with the current, to the shallower landing area.

She had caught just a quick glimpse of Reis Hassan lowering a small reed skiff into the water about half an hour ago, so that he could row the other two men to shore. That was when she'd lain down in her bed and pretended to sleep. In case Sonnebourne or Morgan looked back at the *dahabeeyah*, she didn't want to be caught spying through the window.

Now, as Zoe peered out to survey the glittering moonlit waters, she could make out steps cut into the rock of Philae island, leading upwards into the shadows.

A small, single-masted vessel barely larger than a rowboat lay at anchor about ten yards away.

Presumably, it belonged to whoever Lord Sonnebourne and Mr. Morgan had gone to meet. She didn't believe they actually wanted to see the ruined temple in the moonlight, any more than she would have believed the earth was flat.

Zoe went to the side of Safiya's bed and crouched down.

"Safiya?" she whispered. She took hold of the girl's shoulder and shook her gently, praying that the girl didn't cry out or scream at being woken. And that she could be roused at all.

Safiya's eyes opened and she blinked, her gaze bleary and confused as she struggled to focus on Zoe's face. She murmured something in Arabic, and Zoe's heart contracted at the thought of yet another way this plan could go horribly wrong: she still didn't even know whether or not Safiya spoke any English. If she didn't, Zoe would be no more able to communicate with her than she would with the maid.

"Shhh." Zoe put her fingertips lightly against the girl's mouth, trying not to startle or frighten her. "Do you understand English?"

The wave of relief she felt when Safiya nodded was almost sickening.

"My name is Zoe—" she began, then stopped, wondering how on earth she was going to explain who she was and everything that had happened. The entire time they had been travelling together, Safiya had been either unconscious or too befuddled with the laudanum to take in her surroundings or who was with her. And, looking at their position objectively, she hadn't any more reason to trust Zoe than she did Mrs. Orles.

Safiya interrupted, though, struggling to sit up. "I know who you are."

"You do?"

Safiya nodded again, pushing the loosened tangle of her long dark hair back and giving Zoe a small smile. "I am not always so stupid with the ... what is the word? The medicine—drugs—they give me. Most of the time I am. But other times, I pretend. I hope that they will give me less if they think I am weak and helpless. That maybe I will have the chance to get away."

"That was clever." A tiny spark of hope was flickering inside Zoe's chest. Their odds of success might not be quite so grim as she had thought after all.

"Maybe." Safiya swayed a little as if she were dizzy with the effort of sitting and pressed her hands against her temples. "So far, it has not helped, though. I feel sick all the time, and my head goes around and around when I try to stand, and I am so tired I cannot think ... but I know that you are Zoe Rosario, and that you are a prisoner, like I am." She looked around their moonlit stateroom, still blinking. "Where are we? And why do I feel better tonight?"

"We're on a boat, traveling down the Nile. And you're better because I poured away the drugs Mrs. Orles was giving you and substituted tea, instead. Also I gave Mrs. Orles a dose in her coffee."

"I am glad." Safiya's expression hardened. "She is evil, that one. Although not so evil as the man."

"Lord Sonnebourne?" Zoe wouldn't disagree.

"I do not know his name. He came to my school, where I was studying in England. He said that he had been sent to me by my brother, Selim. He said"—reflexively, her hand went to the scar that ran down one cheek. "He said that he knew of a doctor who could take this away for me. The blond woman was with him. She said that she would go with me, so that it would all be respectable, proper, and I need not fear coming away alone with a man. They brought me to a place—a doctor's surgery, they said. They said that they would give me an injection, and I would sleep, and when I woke, the scar on my face would be gone."

She pressed her eyes closed a moment. "My brother and my father would be so disappointed in me if they knew how foolish I had been. I do not remember any more, except ..." Her brow furrowed. "Except small bits. A train? And a boat?" Her gaze suddenly sharpened, turning more fully aware. "Did you say that we were in *Egypt*?"

"Yes. Lord Sonnebourne has hired a *dahabeeyah* to take us down the Nile. We've just passed Aswan."

Safiya looked as though she were struggling to take everything in. "I do not understand. Why should they bring me back to Egypt? Unless they know—"

"Know what?" Zoe asked.

"Nothing." Safiya pressed her lips together.

Zoe didn't believe her. She'd seen the quick flash of fear cross the girl's expression. But trying to persuade Safiya to confide in her would waste time—time they didn't have.

"Are you feeling well enough to walk?" she asked.

"I think so."

Safiya swung her legs down, but her knees buckled at once when she tried to get to her feet. Zoe caught her, and felt a jolt of fresh alarm at how hot the girl's skin felt. She'd been right that Safiya was running a fever.

"Just rest a moment," Zoe told her. She lowered Safiya back onto the edge of the bunk, her heart hammering. She couldn't hope to carry the girl; Safiya was taller than she was, and if she couldn't even stand on her own—

Safiya struggled to stand again, though, and this time managed, only leaning slightly against Zoe. "I am all right," she gasped. "But how will we get off the boat?"

Zoe had been asking herself that question.

"The crew sleep at the front of the boat, on the deck," she said. "And Lord Sonnebourne and Mr. Morgan have gone, at least for the time being. Can you swim?"

Although even if the answer was yes, she didn't think Safiya would be strong enough to manage.

"I can. But we should not have to," Safiya answered. "I have never sailed on a boat like this one before, but I have seen them. There should be a small … what do you call it? A boat with oars?"

"A rowboat?"

"Yes. One used by the crew to get to shore so that they can buy fresh food and drink along the way."

Zoe's heart quickened. They would still have to rely on an astonishing degree of luck, but at least the thing seemed a fraction more possible.

"Let's go, then. Quickly," she whispered.

Safiya was dressed already; Mrs. Orles never bothered to help her change into night clothes for sleeping. Zoe helped her find her shoes, ignoring the fact that just the effort of bending over to put them on left Safiya breathless.

Safiya stood up, holding Zoe's hand again for support, and they started across the room. Halfway across, a floorboard creaked, sounding loud as a pistol shot to Zoe's keyed-up nerves.

They both froze. Safiya squeezed her eyes shut, and Zoe had to fight the urge to do the same—as though they were children playing at hide-and-seek, hoping that if they couldn't see, they wouldn't be seen, either.

But nothing happened.

Zoe counted to ten, then resumed their stealthy progress across the cabin, reached the door, and eased it open.

Outside, the corridor was dark and silent.

She locked the door from the inside, then pulled it closed after them. When Mrs. Orles woke, she would come along with the key. But it might delay the discovery of their escape by a few hours, if Sonnebourne or Morgan took it into his head to check on them when they returned.

"Come." Zoe led the way towards the back of the boat, where a short flight of steps led up to the small deck at the rear of the cabins.

Safiya had to pause every few steps to rest, leaning against one of the walls, and Zoe fought the urge to beg her to hurry.

Finally, though, they were outside, and peering over the boat's railing to the river below.

The moonlight was brighter out here, making Zoe feel as exposed as if she were standing on a lighted stage. But it also enabled her to see that the rowboat was there, just a few feet below them, tied to the *dahabeeyah* by a length of rough hemp cord.

"I'll go first," Zoe whispered. "Then I can help you."

She hoisted herself up and over the side of the railing, then dropped down, hanging by her hands until her feet touched the wooden planks of the rowboat's bottom. The small vessel rocked alarmingly, threatening to pitch her head first into the water, but she managed to steady herself, planting her feet and bracing her hands against the side of the *dahabeeyah*.

"All right, come ahead," she whispered up to Safiya.

Safiya tried to clamber over the railing as Zoe had done, but she couldn't manage it. Her muscles shook and she fell back onto the deck with a thump that Zoe fully expected to rouse the sleeping crew.

"I cannot." Safiya's eyes were wide and tear-filled in the moonlight. "You should go on without me. At least you will be able to get away."

Zoe shut her eyes for a second, not knowing what to do. If her imaginary version of Sherlock popped up in her mind with advice, she'd be nothing but grateful at this point. But even he was silent.

Apparently even inside her own mind, Sherlock Holmes was maddeningly uncooperative and inconvenient.

"We are both of us getting away." Since she couldn't raise her voice, Zoe made her whisper as fierce as possible. "Either we get safely off this ship together, or neither of us does! Now, try again."

Safiya obeyed, this time managing to pull herself up and over the railing.

"Good." Zoe caught her, prayed to anyone who might be listening that the boat wouldn't capsize under them, and helped Safiya to sit down in the rowboat's narrow hull.

She let her breath out in quick relief, then looked up at the rope that was still keeping them moored fast to the *dahabeeyah*.

"I don't suppose you have a knife?" she murmured to Safiya.

Eyes wide and frightened, the Egyptian girl shook her head.

Zoe didn't have a knife, either. Even if she had thought about trying to secure a weapon of some sort before this—which she hadn't—Mrs. Orles kept all sharp implements well away from their cabin. Greedy and poisonous the housekeeper might be, but she wasn't a fool. Zoe hadn't seen so much as a pair of nail scissors in weeks.

A handicap which you ought to have taken steps to overcome before this, Sherlock's voice commented in her mind.

"Of course, now you decide to start talking to me again," she muttered.

"What?" Safiya gave her a startled look.

"Nothing." Since the only other option was to climb back on board and start ransacking the boat for a knife, Zoe attacked the knot that fastened the rope to the rowboat's mooring ring with her fingernails.

She broke two of her nails, but finally the knot gave way, the rope slipped through the mooring ring, and they were free.

"Where shall we go?" Safiya whispered.

Zoe took hold of the oars—which bumped awkwardly in their wooden crutches—and then hesitated. The sensible, the only logical thing to do was to get as far away from here with as much speed as possible.

But Sonnebourne was meeting with someone, presumably someone important, on the island.

Reason also dictated that Zoe was the only person who could find out the purpose of that meeting, and, moreover, what Sonnebourne was intending to accomplish here in Egypt.

And logic—and her own experience of the man—also stated that if Sonnebourne was allowed to accomplish his purpose here, innocent people would die.

"You can choose," she whispered back to Safiya. "Sonnebourne and Mr. Morgan have an appointment here at Philae. We can try to run away—row for the opposite bank of the river. Or we can go ashore here at the island first, and try to overhear what their meeting is about."

She waited, the beats of her own heart loud in her own ears. A small, cowardly part of her was hoping that Safiya would take the first option, to run.

But almost immediately the Egyptian girl shook her head. "We go ashore here," she whispered back. "If we can, we must find out his plans."

CHAPTER 18: FLYNN

"Here," Becky said. "I found it."

She held up the volume from Mr. Holmes's files she'd been flipping through and read out loud, stumbling a bit over the unfamiliar Egyptian words. "The Urabi revolt, also known as the Urabi Revolution, was a nationalist uprising in Egypt occurring between the years 1879 to 1882. Led by and named for Colonel Ahmed Urabi, the nationalists sought to depose the Khedive Tewfik Pasha and end British and French influence over the Egyptian nation."

"What happened?" Flynn asked.

They'd snuck out of Becky's house all right, without attracting any notice from Constable Polk. Now they were alone in Baker Street, since Mr. Holmes had packed Mrs. Hudson off to visit her sister in the country, where she'd be safe while he was gone.

"I mean, I'm guessing 'Urabi and his fellows didn't win?"

Becky frowned at the page again. "It says here that the uprising was ended by an Anglo-Egyptian War and takeover of the government."

"What about 'Urabi?"

"He was captured and exiled to the Island of Ceylon," Becky said.

"Think he's one of Farooq's lot?" Flynn asked.

"I don't see how he can be, not unless he escaped from Ceylon," Becky said.

"He's important somehow, though. Otherwise Farooq and the other man wouldn't have been talking about him. And Selim wouldn't have turned green just at the mention of his name."

"I know." Becky stood up, putting the volume of Mr. Holmes's files back on the shelf. "And I don't know what it all means—yet. But we need to go to the Diogenes Club. Mycroft can send word to Mr. Holmes about this straight away."

CHAPTER 19: ZOE

One of the men must have brought a lantern from the *dahabeeyah*. Zoe could see the glow of it as, crouching down so far that she almost bent double, she crept up the stone staircase towards the temple ruins.

The oil flame cast sufficient light to reveal, at the top of the steps, a wide courtyard, with shadowy columns on either side and a towering columned building beyond.

Zoe could imagine robed Egyptian figures, lining up to enter the building so that they could worship their animal-headed gods.

But more to the point were the figures of the three men she could see standing amidst the half-broken columns beyond the courtyard.

She could also hear a faint murmur of voices, but she was too far away to catch any words.

She shut her eyes, wondering whether she was inviting disaster if she tried to move closer.

At least she was alone. Safiya had been much too weak to risk making the climb up the stone steps.

Zoe had dragged their rowboat around an outcropping of rock, where it would be well screened from the view of anyone coming down the stairs. Safiya was with it now, in what Zoe hoped would be a safe hiding place.

She edged sideways into the deepest shadows at the edge of the courtyard, praying that she wouldn't send any stones or chunks of rubble clattering in the dark.

One other small circumstance in her favour: the men's night vision would be hampered by the lamp, making it hard for them to see anything beyond their own small circle of illumination.

She took a cautious step, another, and another, pressing herself against the stone pylons and crouching behind half-tumbled down stone walls until she caught a few distinct words.

"The drugs will not harm my men?"

The voice wasn't Morgan's or Sonnebourne's, so it must be that of the third man.

Risking a quick look from around the edge of the column, Zoe could see him, big and broad-chested and wearing a hooded dark robe.

"They need not even take them."

That was Sonnebourne talking.

"The drugs need only be found in the evening rations. Sprinkled liberally, of course, but that need only be done with the rations that remain after the men have eaten. Then they feign sleep. As long as they are to be trusted?"

The hooded man spat on the ground. "They hate the *Englezi*. And some of them have lost homes—farmland—to the construction."

"Fine. But pick one other supervisor, and drug his food, so that he genuinely becomes insensible. Possibly a guard. One you do not like. The charade will be more convincing if you can manage that."

"We understand one another," the hooded man said. He glanced briefly towards the river and the landing steps.

"The twenty-fourth?" Morgan asked.

He sounded nervous, Zoe thought, and he kept glancing around them as though he disliked the ruined temple's atmosphere—or feared they were being observed.

"The twenty-fourth. You have the funds?"

Sonnebourne raised something he was holding in one hand.

A suitcase or satchel, Zoe thought. The clasp gleamed bronze in the lamplight.

"Local currency," Morgan said.

The other man reached for it, but Sonnebourne didn't let go straight away.

"Fail me, and one day I will see you killed. You, and your family, as well. You will watch them die."

The hooded man didn't answer, only took the suitcase and turned on his heel, striding off into the shadows.

After several long moments, Sonnebourne and Morgan followed, passing so close by Zoe's hiding place that she could have put out her hand and touched them.

But neither man noticed.

"Hold up the lantern," Sonnebourne said. "Reis Hassan said he would await our signal to come back for us on his skiff."

"Very well."

Zoe pressed herself more deeply into the shadows as the lantern light swung in a wide arc that thankfully missed her place of concealment, and then the two men kept walking.

As they started down the stone steps, Zoe heard Morgan say,

"You realise how many people will be killed if this scheme comes off?"

Zoe didn't want to risk looking, but the rattle of Sonnebourne's steps paused, as though he'd stopped walking. "I hope, my friend, that you are not developing a conscience at this late date."

His voice was dangerously soft.

"Hardly." Morgan barked a laugh that had an edge of nervousness to it. "I'm thinking about the consequences if we're caught."

"In that case, I suggest you do your utmost to ensure that we are not caught," Sonnebourne said.

They started walking again. Zoe waited until their voices had faded into silence, and then several long minutes more.

She listened all the while for any sound that might mean they'd discovered the rowboat and Safiya, but none came.

At last she crept to the top of the stairs and looked down. Reis Hassan had indeed come to fetch them; the moonlight showed the reed skiff gliding back over the still waters to the *dahabeeyah*, with Sonnebourne and Morgan on board.

Zoe watched them climb back onto the deck of the sailing vessel. Then she picked up her skirts and ran down the stone flight of steps as quickly as she dared.

CHAPTER 20: FLYNN

"Something's wrong—something's happened," Becky said.

Their cab had just rolled up within sight of the Diogenes Club, and Flynn could see that even though it was barely seven o'clock in the morning, there was a crowd of people outside the white-columned entrance. Some of them were wearing the livery uniform of the Diogenes club servants. Some looked like passers-by who'd just come to see what all the commotion was about.

Several wore the blue uniforms and helmets of policemen.

A sick, cold feeling sprouted in the pit of Flynn's stomach. He shoved some money at their cab driver and then jumped down, not even waiting for the driver to give him change or for Becky to scramble down.

He knew she'd be right behind him anyway.

He raced towards the entrance, elbowing his way through the crowd.

"What's going on?" he asked the fellow next to him, when he'd shoved his way as far towards the front of the mob as he could get.

It wasn't easy to be heard. Everyone else was pushing and shoving and talking, too—and up closer to the Diogenes club building, a couple of the policemen were trying to hold back the crowd and telling them to move along.

The man Flynn had asked looked like a city gent: morning coat, top hat, lemon-coloured gloves, and shiny gaiters on his shoes. He had a monocle on a gold chain and a long, horsey kind of face. Probably belonged to the Diogenes Club—and he was definitely the type who wouldn't ordinarily give Flynn the time of day. But right now he also looked like something had scared him badly enough that he wasn't paying too much attention to who he talked to.

"One of the club members here was shot, just as we were coming out of the front entrance." His eyes had a kind of dazed look. "I was standing just beside him when it happened. A shot from an unknown gunman across the street, we must assume, but … a few inches to the right, and I might have been the one …" His Adam's apple bobbed as he swallowed. "They're just loading him into an ambulance and taking him away to hospital now."

The sick feeling in Flynn's stomach had grown a whole lot worse. "One of the club members? Do you know his name?"

The question seemed to bring the toff back to himself and make him remember who he was and the fact that he might pay Flynn a half shilling to polish his boots for him, but that was all.

He peered down at Flynn through his monocle. "Really, I fail to see how that can be any business of yours. Now be off with you!"

He made a shooing motion with one gloved hand, then turned away.

Flynn gritted his teeth. He would have picked the blighter's pocket, but he was too busy trying to get a look through the crowd, to where he now could see an ambulance carriage drawn up at the foot of the wide granite front steps.

As Flynn kept pushing his way forwards, the people in front of him parted just enough that he got a better look at what was happening. A bulky, familiar form was being loaded onto a stretcher. Flynn got a look at the man's face and pulled in his breath.

It was Mr. Mycroft. Not that he hadn't been almost sure all along, but it was worse, somehow, seeing him with the shoulder of his coat all bloodied and his face looking pale as death.

Unless he really was dead?

Flynn's heart started trying to pound out of his chest at that thought, and he started shoving through the crowd harder. He got some dirty looks, but he ignored them. Don't be dead, please don't be dead …

Just as the stretcher was being loaded into the back of the ambulance, Flynn saw Mr. Mycroft's eyelids flutter a bit, and his hand move. Not much, but he was still alive.

Flynn's breath went out in a rush. But then he saw something else, something that made him feel like he'd not only been kicked in the gut, but had a bucket full of ice water dumped down the back of his neck, too. The driver of the ambulance wagon was a big chap with broad shoulders, and the hands that held the horse's reins were huge and strong-looking. He gave the reins a flick and the horses started to move, pulling the wagon away from the Club. The man looked back—and that was when Flynn's heart stopped, because he'd seen the man before.

Tall and strong, with blond hair.

He hadn't been able to give Mr. Holmes much of a description before, but now that he was seeing the man again, he was certain of it: the ambulance driver was the same man who'd met with Farooq at the place where the Sons of Ra had cached their weapons.

CHAPTER 21: WATSON

"You are witnessing the greatest construction enterprise ever undertaken by mankind," said Lord Kitchener.

His voice rang with pride and even awe. Handsome-featured, with his dark hair parted at the centre, he wore a walrus moustache and maintained such a rigid posture that he put me in mind of a child's carved wooden nutcracker soldier, though a far more serious and imposing one.

Lucy and I were standing with Kitchener on an observation platform above the waters of the mighty Nile River, looking towards its opposite bank, more than a mile away from us and too far for us to see.

"An enormous enterprise," Lucy said.

"The work will take two or three more years," Kitchener went on, with a trace of an Irish accent. "It will dwarf the pyramids, the great wall of China, and all the seven wonders of the world."

In Cairo, before our departure, Holmes had directed us that upon our arrival at Aswan, we were to meet Kitchener at the site of the great dam that was being built here, but he had not told us why.

118 ⌕ ANNA ELLIOTT AND CHARLES VELEY

This morning we had obtained rooms at the Old Cataract, the newly opened hotel Thomas Cook had built atop a high granite cliff within a short walk of the city of Aswan. But inquiring at the desk had revealed no messages for either Lucy or me.

I could only assume, however, that Holmes thought the incomplete dam was a likely point of attack for Sonnebourne and the Kaiser's forces. And what Kitchener was saying seemed to confirm this assumption.

At age 49, Kitchener had earned his baronial title by ruthlessly suppressing the Sudanese invasion in a conclusive victory barely one year ago. Now, as British military commander for all Egypt, he fairly brimmed over with suppressed energy as he continued, his head held high.

"Indeed, at least two million pounds and all Britain's prestige are at risk here in this remote river valley. If we fail, Egypt will be lost, and with it the Suez Canal and England's control of the entire Mediterranean."

"Stunning to contemplate," Lucy said.

She gestured downwards, towards the tumult of construction activity below. There, easily one hundred fifty feet below us, thousands of men and dozens of great machines were carving an enormously wide and open channel into the great riverbed.

The width of the channel itself was stunning enough, for it spread out before us for nearly two hundred feet. The yawning chasm was crisscrossed with wood-slatted footbridges, sloping downwards from the near edge and then upwards to the opposite edge, each footbridge supporting workmen in their travels down into the great pit beneath and back up again. But the depth of the great gorge was still more unsettling.

I made the mistake of looking down to the bottom, and felt a dizzying surge of vertigo. Lucy caught my arm.

"Steady on," she said quietly, holding me upright.

My pride would not permit me to look away just then, but I was grateful for her support.

Below us, men appeared almost as small as insects as they swarmed over the dun-coloured surface of the exposed earth, raising clouds of dust. Each man was active, pounding or digging or cutting into the dirt and granite bed rock, or moving newly cut granite blocks, or shifting dirt and mud into baskets and wheel barrows.

White robes and white Egyptian caps predominated among the men, while here and there Europeans were visible in their white pith helmets and khaki attire. All were engaged in forcing a trench through the granite bed rock and building up a new wall within it.

Finally, I stepped back from the edge of the platform.

"Mind your footing, Dr. Watson," Kitchener said. "You don't want to be falling onto those fellows, and they don't want you down there."

I nodded, still trying to take in all the myriad of activity before me. It was difficult to believe what I was seeing with my own eyes.

On our left a great wall of timber rose up from a foundation of concrete, crushed stone, and gravel held together with Portland cement. At the base of the timber and concrete, granite blocks were being set into place by workmen with winches and tackle.

On our right was an even higher wall, with an enormous high platform built upon great tall timbers, like supporting columns inside of a high cathedral. Atop this platform, the towers of three gigantic lifting cranes hung over the great trench like a giant's fishing-poles over a dry river. Between the platforms, and creating a nearly palpable din, were three steam shovels. Two were scraping and lifting the residue from the dry river bed. The third manoeuvred new loads of crushed rock newly deposited from the buckets of the lifting cranes. Billowing coal smoke rose from these huge mechanical beasts. Their loads, when dumped, added to the din with a booming crash, punctuated by cries and shouts from the men working along the floor and up and down the cliff-like reddish-pink granite rock.

Lucy's gaze moved from top to bottom of the great crater. "Reminds me of a painting I once saw—an artist's vision of Dante's Inferno," she said.

"Not for long," said Kitchener. "In a month, what you see between the timbers will be a solid mass of concrete and granite, a wall one hundred fifty feet deep and one hundred fifty feet thick. At the base, of course. That base goes down fifty feet into the granite bed rock. Three hundred Italian stone cutters do that work."

"What happens after a month?" I asked.

"After the concrete has hardened and the sluice gates are functional, we move on. First, we extend the earthen protective barrier—that huge pile of dirt you can just see beyond that wall on your right. Without that protection, no further excavation is possible. But once that protection is in place, we can push forward. A hundred yards at a push, and so onward and onward. We will not stop until we have gone all the way to the eastern bank, which you can barely see, since it is more than a mile away."

"Dizzying to contemplate," said Lucy. Evidently, she was also having thoughts about an attack from Sonnebourne, for she asked, "Has there been any trouble with the Egyptian part of the work force? In Cairo, we heard some talk of rebellion."

Kitchener raised one shoulder. "No more than is to be expected. Ten thousand men work here in this small space. Some are skilled, like the three hundred stonecutters, and relatively civilized and obedient. Most are not. There are fights, and there are always those troublemakers who instigate hatred for the British." His lips quirked in a wry smile. "But so far their efforts have not been sufficient to overcome the desire to earn an honest wage."

"And the soldiers under your command keep order?" Lucy asked.

"They do."

"Could an enemy dynamite the earthen barrier?" Lucy asked.

Kitchener gave her a quizzical look. "I doubt very much that they would succeed in doing much damage. The natural tendency of the rift would be for gravity to heal it. The earth would simply cave in to plug the gap. I must ask whether you have any information that would suggest such a plan of attack?"

I was uncertain what reply Holmes would wish me to make to that question; he had not specified whether anyone—even a man so highly placed as Kitchener—ought to be taken into our confidence.

Remembering the carnage I had witnessed in Afghanistan, I asked, "What of a cannon of some sort? A howitzer? A machine gun?"

Kitchener gave me a look that was at once sympathetic and condescending. "You were at Maiwand, weren't you?" he asked.

"I was."

"I respect your service, Doctor. But I assure you that an artillery attack is precisely the offense that my men are trained to prevent. No weapon of that size could be smuggled into Egypt, in the first place, and there is no position here where it could be installed that is not under our constant scrutiny. You can rest easy on that point."

"One other question," Lucy said. "Have you had any difficulties with snakes? Do you have a need for antivenin?"

"Not much worry about snakes. The Egyptians are used to them and the others of us have boots. Actually, our chief difficulty here is with socks."

Lucy's brows edged upwards. "Socks?"

"They don't wear well in this hot dusty climate. The men have trouble. You know Napoleon said an army travels on its stomach, but they all need to use their feet. And when the socks go bad, the feet follow. And so goes the man."

"For want of a nail, the horse was lost, and so on," said Lucy.

Kitchener seemed delighted with her observation. "Same principle exactly! Horses and men are similar."

"Will the men work as usual Christmas Eve?" Lucy asked.

"Best to keep them busy."

"So on the 24th all those men—"

"Will be down there, working. They are here to bring home their pay to their families."

Lucy asked, "And will there be work performed on the Christmas holiday?"

"We shall observe the holiday on Christmas. We will have a celebration at the barracks. There's a time for celebration, as the Good Book says. A time for every purpose under the heaven. You are most welcome to come."

"If we have something to celebrate, we will," I said. "Thank you for your time, Lord Kitchener."

We turned away, making our way across the dusty path that would eventually lead us back to the point where we had tethered the hired donkeys who had carried us to the construction site.

"Well, that was informative," Lucy said. Her cheeks were flushed with the heat, and she sounded more discouraged than I had yet heard her. "It's unlikely that Sonnebourne could destroy the dam with a bomb or attack the workers with a direct show of force, and even snakes don't seem to present much of a problem. Unless he plans to steal their supply of socks, I don't see that we're any further along in the investigation than before."

I could not help but agree, but I said, attempting to speak cheeringly, "Let us return to the hotel. Perhaps Holmes will have sent a message by now."

"We ought to have a look around the area, as well," Lucy said. "According to what Dr. Olfrig told us, Lord Sonnebourne planned to journey to Aswan. But so far, we've seen no sign of him."

Inquiries at the hotel and amongst the porters and souvenir-sellers who thronged the banks of the river had produced no reports of a man answering Sonnebourne's description, or of a *dahabeeyah* that might have been hired by him.

We had heard nothing of Zoe, either. Lucy did not say as much, but I was certain the thought was in her mind.

"If he does intend mischief here, he would hardly sail boldly up to the city and book a room at a Thomas Cook hotel," I said.

"No." Lucy glanced back over her shoulder at the organised chaos of the construction site we had just left behind. "We have to find him. You heard what Kitchener said about the outcome if the project fails—England will lose access to the Suez Canal, and our position of strength in the whole Mediterranean will be demolished. Can you imagine anything that the Kaiser would like more?"

CHAPTER 22: FLYNN

Becky caught up to him before he'd gone more than a dozen yards.

"Why are we running after the ambulance?"

"The driver—saw him—met with Farooq." Flynn hadn't got the breath to say any more and still run fast enough to keep the ambulance in sight.

Becky's eyes widened, and then she was pelting down the street in step with him.

Turn—turn again—luckily the streets were crowded with people doing last-minute Christmas shopping, and he and Becky could blend in with the crowds. They got a lot of dirty looks from people they accidentally bumped into, but Flynn didn't think the blond-haired ambulance driver had noticed them.

Up ahead, the carriage turned again to drive through Mayfair.

"Where are they taking him?" Becky gasped.

Flynn shook his head. His lungs were on fire and his feet felt like they were going to fall off if he had to run another step. But then a block or so up ahead of them, the ambulance slowed down, turned, and drove through the tall, curly wrought-iron gates of a big brick place that stood on the corner of Hertford Street.

Flynn looked at Becky, questioning, and she nodded.

They walked towards the place, trying to look casual about it.

This area of London was even more posh than the Diogenes Club, filled with places that looked like palaces and were big enough to fit a hundred families inside and still have room to spare. There was a short drive up to the house, with trees on either side. The wrought-iron fence went all the way around the property, as far as Flynn could see.

"Sonnebourne has a nasty sense of humour, if he's the one who organised this," Becky said.

"How d'you mean?"

"He probably suspected Mr. Holmes staged that accident in Piccadilly—and now he's just kidnapped Mr. Holmes' brother with another fake ambulance. Like the one Mr. Holmes had Lucy and Dr. Watson drive to get him away." Becky turned, looking up and down the street. "We need to find out exactly what this place is."

It was starting to snow: big fat white flakes that landed on Flynn's face, stuck in his eyelashes, and dripped cold down the back of his neck.

But there was a delivery boy a few doors down, carrying a heavy stack of parcels.

"Oi!" Flynn jogged over to him.

The other boy turned around, blinking through the dark and the snow.

"What's that building there?" Flynn pointed at the big brick house behind the gates. "Do you know who owns it?"

The delivery boy shrugged. "Dunno who owns it, but it's a place for folks as have gone batty."

"Loonies, you mean?"

"That's right. Only since they're rich folks, they call 'em nerve patients," the delivery boy said. He shifted his load of parcels awkwardly. "That all? 'Cause I've got to be getting along."

"That's all. And thank you," Becky said.

"We need to go to Scotland Yard," Flynn said, when the boy had gone off. "Tell your brother about this, or some other copper if he's not there."

Becky gave him a disbelieving look. Flynn wouldn't have believed he'd actually be suggesting going to a police station, either, if he hadn't heard the words just come out of his mouth. But he was scared. He didn't often admit that, even to himself, but there was a cold, tight feeling in his chest, like a thread about to snap.

"You're right," Becky said. She looked scared, too. "But one of us should stay here. You know, just in case they move Mr. Mycroft somewhere else."

"I'll stay. They know you at Scotland Yard," Flynn said. "They're more likely to listen to you."

"All right." Becky looked up and down the street again, which was unhelpfully empty. Flynn would stick out here like a sore thumb. "Let's go around the back. We'll find a good spot for you to hide and then I'll go."

Flynn shoved his hands in his pockets and tried to look like he was just out for a morning stroll—which wasn't easy when he was half frozen and the pavement was already half an inch deep in slush.

They walked around the corner. "Why do you think they'd bring Mr. Mycroft here?"

Becky blew on her hands. "I suppose it makes sense. They shot him before kidnapping him, so they'd need to take him someplace where they could make sure he got medical treatment. Because they didn't want to kill him."

She was right. If they'd wanted Mr. Mycroft dead, they wouldn't have bothered having an ambulance ready to drive him here. So they must want him alive for something.

The soles of Flynn's boots both had holes in them and the slush was coming in, freezing his toes. But he barely noticed it. He had a bad feeling that he knew why they'd want Mr. Mycroft alive.

The snow was picking up, making it hard to see. But he could make out bars on all the lower-level windows of the brick house, and a lot of the upper ones, as well.

"Look, there's another gate here at the back—" Becky started to say, then stopped.

Flynn froze, too, momentarily forgetting about the snow and the cold. A carriage had just pulled up to the back gate, and a couple of men had hopped out.

One unlocked the gate and pushed it open, and the other one dragged the third passenger of the carriage out and started to push him towards the back entrance.

There was a lantern hanging over the back door, so that even through the swirling snow, Flynn got a look at the third man's face.

It was Selim.

CHAPTER 23: FLYNN

One of Selim's eyes was swollen and he had blood running down his chin. He was stumbling along, looking barely aware of where he was going—probably because of the beating he'd clearly gotten.

The two men shoved Selim through the back door and shut it behind them with a bang.

Flynn swallowed hard, feeling like his feet had just been glued to the pavement.

He might not have moved for who knew how long, but Becky grabbed hold of his arm, dragging him away at a run.

"Come on!"

It was several blocks before he realised that they weren't heading in the direction of Scotland Yard, and that they'd just passed by the Savile Row.

"Where are we going? Why aren't we telling the police about this?"

"Don't you see?" Becky's hair was wet, plastered to her face with melted snow, and her lips were starting to turn blue with cold. "We *can't* go to the police! If they've got Selim, that means that something must have happened to Constable Polk. They got past him, and took Selim. Constable Polk is an experienced officer, *and* he was on the lookout for any trouble. How do you think anyone would manage to get past his guard and attack him?"

Flynn saw where she was heading, and he didn't at all like it. But he could follow the line of reasoning just as well as she could. "He'd have trusted someone he knew—another police officer."

"Exactly. We already know that Sonnebourne had police constables working for him—Dr. Watson was attacked by one in Lavender Hill. And Jack won't be back at Scotland Yard, not yet. What happens if we go there, and we pick the wrong person to tell about all of this? Or if whoever we tell tells someone else, someone who's in Sonnebourne's pay?"

Flynn nodded. The cold feeling inside him was getting worse, and he would have loved to find someone else to take charge. Trying to rescue Mr. Mycroft and stop a bombing plot felt far too big a job to tackle on their own. But he could also see Becky's point.

"So what do we do?"

Becky wiped melted snow from her eyes. "We rescue Mycroft ourselves. But first we have to send a telegram to Mr. Holmes. He gave me an address in Aswan where they'd pass any messages on to him. Just in case"—her voice wobbled a bit, but she firmed her chin and went on—"in case things go wrong and something happens to us, he needs to know what we've found out about Farooq mentioning Ahmed Urabi."

CHAPTER 24: ZOE

With her back propped up against a rough block of granite, Zoe tried not to fall asleep. What time was it? Two o'clock in the morning? Three?

She'd already made the discovery that however hot the climate of Egypt was during the day, the nights could turn cold. She shivered and wished she had a watch or some other way of telling time. No, strike that. If a convenient genie happened to pop up from the ancient ruins behind her, offering to grant wishes, she wouldn't waste one of them on a wristwatch.

They were still on the island of Philae. She had watched Morgan and Sonnebourne depart, returning to the *dahabeeyah* on Reis Hassan's skiff. She had held her breath, then, fear filling her entire body as she waited to see whether anyone would notice the missing rowboat that she and Safiya had taken.

But likely thanks to the dark and Sonnebourne's probable insistence that they hurry, no one apparently had.

The *dahabeeyah* had pulled up its anchor and moved off, slipping quietly through the dark waters of the Nile and vanishing into the night.

Her absence and that of Safiya would be discovered eventually. That was a certainty. Zoe hoped they might have until morning, but she couldn't count on it. And when their escape was discovered, she doubted Sonnebourne would have to think very hard about where to start his search.

Safiya, probably still suffering the lingering effects of all the opium, had fallen asleep and was huddled in the bottom of the rowboat. While she slept, Zoe had scrambled over a good deal of the island, exploring as best she could in the dark and trying to formulate some sort of plan.

They couldn't stay here, although there were plenty of places amongst the ruins where they could hide. But a thorough search would doubtless reveal them. She could make out a few mud huts of a village on the east bank, amongst a grove of palm trees. But she doubted her own ability to row the boat that far, especially in the dark. The short trip from the *dahabeeyah* to the island had been enough to prove that rowing a boat against a strong current was a good deal harder than it looked.

Their best option so far as Zoe could see was to make for the nearby island on the western side of Philae—a rugged, mountainous shape barely visible in the dark, it was divided from Philae by a channel so narrow that she could hear the occasional bleat of a goat from the village there.

As soon as it was light enough that the village inhabitants would be awake, she would rouse Safiya and help her across the channel—surely they could swim that far—and beg help from the villagers. It wasn't perhaps the most comprehensive of plans, but at least Safiya spoke the language; she would be able to explain what they needed—

Zoe started in alarm, her heart skipping at a sound from somewhere close by: the roll of a pebble, dislodged by someone's foot.

At least, she thought that was what she'd heard. She held her breath, feeling as though her insides had been scooped out and replaced with clumps of ice. Maybe it had only been a bird, or some other night animal …

No, they were human footsteps, and approaching the small rocky cove where she and Safiya were hidden.

Heart hammering, Zoe stooped, feeling about on the ground, and picked up a solid chunk of rock. Not much of a weapon, but the best she could do.

She held very still, nerves stretching as she listened to the footsteps come closer … closer still … and then stop.

A familiar voice spoke.

"While I generally approve of precautionary measures, it will delay our departure considerably if you club me over the head."

For one wild moment, Zoe thought that the strain had been too much for her over-tired brain, and that she had gone from imagined conversations with Sherlock to actually hallucinating his presence here.

But then he stepped closer, near enough that a shaft of moonlight fell on the familiar outlines of his sharp, hawk-like features.

He glanced at Safiya, still asleep in the rowboat, and nodded. "Ah, she is with you. That is fortunate."

What was also fortunate, Zoe thought, was that she hadn't made the mistake of expecting any heartfelt declarations of relief at Holmes's having found them. His expression, too, was familiar: the impenetrable calm, the gaze that gave rather less away than if he'd been wearing the smoked glasses favoured by scarlet fever victims.

Although she thought there was a faint—a very faint—tension about the edges of his mouth that might mean he was angry. He probably would be angry with her, she thought, even if he would never be human enough to admit it. Angry that she'd let herself be taken captive. For demanding to take part in the investigation that had brought them all here.

She swallowed and managed to find her voice. "What are you doing here?"

Holmes's brows hitched up a fraction of an inch at the question. "I credit your ingenuity enough that I assumed you would attempt an escape at some point in the journey. I have been following Sonnebourne's route, attempting to catch up to you. Asking questions amongst the locals here produced the knowledge that lights had been seen on this island earlier tonight, which led me to assume that Sonnebourne must have scheduled an assignation here. Since those circumstances would have given you your best opportunity to escape, I concluded it probable that you would have seized the chance and attempted to get away. As I see you have done."

Zoe opened her mouth, then closed it again, trying to decide whether to be relieved or offended that Holmes could predict her movements with enough accuracy that her every thought must be an open book to him.

He would undoubtedly say that particular debate was immaterial. Her own feelings about Holmes didn't matter; what mattered was getting them all safely off this island before Sonnebourne returned.

"My only uncertainty was whether you would have been able to engineer Miss Todros's escape along with your own,"

Holmes went on. "But I see you have accomplished that, also. Well done."

He evidently had his temper well under control again, and it was the final two words—uttered in the tone of voice he might have used for praising one of his irregulars—that made Zoe forget the resolve to ignore her own feelings.

"Having allowed yourself that incredibly effusive show of emotion, would you care to tell me what you think our next move should be?"

Holmes's brows rose again, and she let out her breath. She should know that remarks like that where Holmes was concerned were a waste of energy.

"I would suggest first of all that we allow the current to carry the boat you purloined from Sonnebourne's dahabeeyah away from here," Holmes said. "If they find it several miles downriver, it may confuse their attempts to search. We can depart in the boat I used to come ashore, which is moored on the western side of the island."

"Fine," Zoe said.

She crouched down, taking hold of Safiya's shoulder and gently shaking her awake.

"Safiya?"

The girl's big dark eyes looked up at her, dazed.

"A ... A friend of mine has found us," Zoe said. "He's going to help us get away from here, but you'll need to get up and come with us to his boat."

Whether it was the accumulated effects of the drugs given her or sheer, simple exhaustion, Zoe didn't know, but Safiya didn't argue or even ask any questions. With Zoe's help, she obediently stood up and climbed out of the rowboat, though she sat down again almost at once on a boulder.

Holmes shoved the rowboat off the patch of rocky shoreline and then several feet more out into the current. It bobbed and bumped, then was carried away.

Holmes splashed back to them.

He was wearing Egyptian dress, Zoe noted: a long striped robe, belted at the waist by a length of camel-hair rope, and sandals.

"We had best make haste," he said. "I would estimate that we have anywhere between one and four hours before your escape is discovered, and it would be as well to be as far away from here as possible when that discovery occurs."

He still sounded as though he were commenting on the weather or asking Mrs. Hudson to bring him a second cup of tea.

Zoe opened her mouth, then closed it again.

She'd learned a long time ago that it was pointless to blame Holmes for the way his mind worked. Not only pointless, but unfair, even.

Sherlock Holmes had never represented himself to be anything like an ordinary man; he was simply not made that way. The famous Egyptian Sphynx was positively chatty and communicative compared to Holmes.

She put an arm around Safiya, helping the girl to stand. "You lead and we'll follow," she said.

With Holmes in the lead, they skirted their way around the edge of the island.

Philae's history must have been a long and fascinating one. The moon's silver light was enough to show the lotus columns and ruined bas-reliefs of Egyptian animal-headed gods, occasionally even with fragments of the original blue and green and yellow paint remaining—and among them, Zoe saw occasional inscriptions in Greek, and a carved Greek cross that made her think the temples here must have once been adopted and adapted into a place of Christian worship.

And maybe one day, when she wasn't terrified, exhausted, and half frozen by the cold night breeze blowing off the river, she would come back in order to appreciate them.

Tonight, she hadn't much attention to spare. She had to help Safiya, who kept stumbling, while also keeping her own footing on the broken and uneven ground—and she was so preoccupied that when Holmes stopped, she almost walked straight into him, and only caught herself about an inch from his back.

"What is it?" she whispered.

Holmes had stiffened, his head lifting as though he were listening, although Zoe heard nothing at all save the soft lap of the waves on the shore and the occasional trill of a night bird.

The crack of the gun was so sudden, so alien in the night stillness that it took a moment for Zoe to even process what it was—and by that time, Holmes had already been spun sideways by the bullet's impact and collapsed on the ground.

CHAPTER 25: FLYNN

"I think it's dark enough now," Flynn said.

He and Becky were sitting at a corner table in a grubby fish and chips shop across the street from Hyde Park—the only place they'd been able to find where they could keep out of the cold and the snow and not attract too much attention.

They'd had to buy a couple of portions of fried fish and soggy chips, which they weren't even pretending to eat anymore. But at least the owner of the place was willing to leave them alone, especially since there weren't any other customers.

Becky turned to look through the shop's window at the street outside. It was almost night, and Flynn's skin was crawling with impatience to get back to the sanatorium. But they'd talked it over and agreed that they didn't have much choice but to wait until nightfall.

Their odds of getting into the place without being caught weren't any that Flynn would have put money on. But trying it during the daylight hours would have shrunk those odds down to nil.

"All right," Becky said.

She got up, pushing away her newspaper wrapped parcel of food. Flynn folded his packet back up and stuffed it into his pocket.

"What?" He shrugged in answer to Becky's look. "No sense letting it go to waste."

There were lots of times he'd been hungry enough that cold fish and soggy chips would have sounded like a feast.

It was still snowing as they trudged back towards Hertford Street. Every carriage that rolled past splattered them with the freezing cold slush that sprayed off the wheels.

"Think Mr. Holmes got the telegram we sent him?" Flynn asked.

"I hope so." Becky bit her lip. "Jack can't have got the one I sent him, though, or he'd already be here."

That had been Becky's idea, to send a second telegram off to her brother at Scotland Yard. She'd written the message in code so that only Jack would be able to read it, and she'd told him where they were and what had happened.

"What's this murder case he was called out on, anyway?" Flynn asked.

"I don't know, Jack isn't allowed to tell me any details. But I overheard him on the telephone, when the call came in, and the dispatcher on the other end said something about the dead man being one of the guards at the Palace of Westminster."

Flynn frowned, because an idea was tugging at the back of his mind, and staying just out of reach when he tried to think about what it was.

They'd reached the big iron gates of the sanatorium, though.

"What do you think—around back?" he asked.

Becky looked up and down the street. There weren't many

pedestrians about, not in this kind of weather, but there were still carriages rolling past, carrying all the rich people who lived nearby to and from their fancy teas and dinner parties.

She nodded. "Good idea. What do we do when we get there?"

"Try to climb over?"

The iron railing was well over the top of Flynn's head. But whoever had designed it hadn't been trying very hard to keep out intruders, because it had curly bits all over it that would make for decent foot holds.

As soon as they'd rounded the corner behind the sanatorium, Flynn jumped and caught one of the bars near the top of the railing.

There was a big-ish square of lawn here, with some evergreen trees that would screen them from the view of anyone in the house.

He planted his boot on the fence and started to pull himself up.

Woof!

Behind the iron fence, a huge dog—even bigger than Becky's Prince and a whole lot meaner—lunged at him, barking and snarling and showing a mouthful of yellow teeth that each looked the size of one of Flynn's pinky fingers.

Flynn bit his tongue trying not to yell, let go of the railing, and sprang back, his heart hammering.

So that explained why they weren't too worried about people climbing the fence.

At least no one else came out to investigate, and the dog had stopped barking now that Flynn was off the fence.

Flynn gulped down a shaky breath and pulled the packet of fish and chips he'd saved out from his pocket.

"Here, boy. Good dog."

He took out one of the chips and crouched down, inching back towards the fence with his hand holding the food outstretched.

Becky stared at him. "What are you doing? You hate dogs!"

"Yeah, well, I'm not too keen on the idea of Selim and Mr. Mycroft being stuck in there, either, with whoever's kidnapped them."

Flynn inched a step closer and tossed the chip through the iron fence railing. The dog caught it in mid-air, the huge teeth chomped, and the chip was gone.

Flynn swallowed, trying not to think about what those teeth could do to his ankle or leg. "The good news is we know he's hungry."

"If that's the good news, we're in serious trouble." Becky *didn't* hate dogs, but even she looked a bit shaken.

Flynn tossed the big animal another chip and took another step closer.

Four chips later and he was standing right next to the fence while the dog eyed the packet in his hands eagerly.

"You go first," he told Becky. "I'll keep him busy while you get over."

Becky nodded, hitching up her skirt and starting to climb.

Flynn broke off a chunk of fried fish.

"Better hurry," he told Becky.

The fish was disappearing at an alarming rate.

"Oh, do you really think so?" Becky hissed back. She was at the top of the fence, now, wobbling unsteadily as she tried to swing over the spikes at the top. "All right, come on."

She managed to get over, then dropped down onto the grass on the other side.

The dog bumped his nose against the railing and growled.

Apparently Flynn wasn't being quick enough with the food, although at least the animal didn't seem to mind Becky being inside.

"All right, here." Bundling up the remaining fish and chips, Flynn threw the parcel as hard as he could, far across the square of lawn.

The dog galloped after it—and Flynn swarmed up the fence faster than he'd ever climbed anything in his life.

He tore a gash in his coat as he got over the spikes at the top, but dropped down onto the ground beside Becky, panting.

"Now what?" he whispered.

The dog was tearing open the newspaper-wrapped food, but it wouldn't keep him busy for long.

"Try to get in the back door?"

The rear entrance where they'd seen the two men drag Selim in was just ahead.

"That won't work." Flynn shook his head. "How do we know someone's not waiting on the other side of the door, ready to grab us the second we step through?"

"Fine." Becky wiped the melting snow from her eyes. "Look, there aren't any bars on that window up there."

She was right, most of the windows had bars over them. But there was one on the second floor just above their heads that didn't.

It was dark inside, too. Some of the windows had lights on—especially on the ground floor—but this one was just a square of empty black.

Becky looked up at the evergreen that stood next to the house. "Do you think the tree branches will hold us?"

"I think it's a toss-up between that and being turned into the second course of the dog's dinner."

The big animal had finished shredding the newspaper and gulping down the last scraps of food and now it was coming back towards them, growling deep in its throat.

"You'd think it would be grateful to us for feeding it. Prince would have been."

Becky jumped, caught hold of a low-hanging tree branch, and pulled herself up. Flynn followed, clambering up through the snowy branches until they were perched on one just outside the unbarred window.

Becky tried to pry up the window, then stopped. "It's stuck—or locked."

"What?" Flynn was trying not to look down at the dog, which was circling around the bottom of the tree.

Any second now and it would decide to start barking—and then someone would come out to see what all the noise was about.

She gave him a look. "Do you need a dictionary? *Locked* means it won't open."

"Here, let me try."

Flynn took out his pen knife and wedged it in between the window frame and the glass, fiddling until he felt the lock snap.

He shoved the sash open. He'd meant to have a look inside the room first, to make sure it was safe, but he lost his balance and tumbled head first into the room, landing with a thud on the carpeted floor.

He hadn't managed to get his breath back before a voice from somewhere in the room's dark shadows spoke.

"Visitors for Christmas?" the voice said. "How *very* nice!"

CHAPTER 26: ZOE

Safiya screamed. Zoe had just presence of mind enough to drag her down to the ground where she would be a less easy target. Then she scrambled over to kneel beside Holmes. For a heart-stopping moment, she thought that he'd been killed by the shot.

"Sherlock?" she gasped. "Sherlock, are you—"

He moved, rolling over with a sound that would have been a groan if his tightly compressed lips hadn't contained it.

"I seem to have underestimated the minimum amount of time … before your escape would be discovered." It took him two breaths to get the words out.

"Believe it or not, I had actually reached that very same conclusion!" Zoe snapped.

Fear sharpened her voice. She was straining her ears to listen, but she couldn't hear anything above the thud of her own heart.

At least there were no more shots.

"How badly are you hurt?" she demanded.

She could already see a spreading stain on the sleeve and shoulder of his cotton robe.

Holmes struggled to sit up. "A flesh wound … to the deltoid muscle." He squinted with the effort of peering down his nose at his bloodied shoulder. "Although it may have nicked the triceps brachii, as well, in which case—"

Zoe interrupted, speaking through gritted teeth. "If you are about to deliver a pedantic, over-educated lecture on anatomy, you will no longer have to worry about our shooter, because I will murder you myself."

Holmes let out another muffled grunt of pain as he moved again, trying to untie the string that cinched the neckline of the Egyptian robe. "The bullet may have damaged the deltoid branch of the thoracoacromial artery. In which case, stopping the bleeding is a matter of some urgency, since it could lead to loss of consciousness or possibly life."

Save for the slight raggedness as he struggled to get his breath back, his tone of voice changed not at all.

Zoe didn't trust herself to answer, since it was even odds that she would either hit him or do something still more irrational, such as start to cry.

So she clamped her lips together and turned, trying to decide where on this barren and rocky island she would find anything to help.

"Here." Safiya had crept forwards and now handed over the scarf, which she'd just unwrapped from around her head. "You can use this to slow the bleeding."

"Thank you."

Zoe pressed it tightly against Holmes's shoulder, which earned her a harshly indrawn breath, but at least no more anatomy lectures.

"I believe I can manage," Holmes said after a moment. "If you would—"

He cut off abruptly, and a second later, Zoe heard it, too: the dry crunch of footsteps moving towards them through the dark.

Holmes motioned sharply for silence, but Zoe couldn't have made a sound even if she had tried. Her heart was lodged firmly up in her throat and her mouth had gone as parched as the Egyptian desert sand.

They were skirting around the edge of a temple courtyard, outlined with vast lotus columns stretching up to the night sky. Zoe would have thought Holmes scarcely capable of moving, but he sprang to his feet, swaying only briefly before he drew back into the shadow of one of the columns.

Zoe started to rise, too, but he motioned sharply for her to stay where she was, and she subsided, biting her lip.

Holmes was maddening and arrogant and insufferably self-sufficient. But she had also never known him to take an unnecessary risk or plunge recklessly into danger. The very thought was laughable, when his every move was calculated almost to the millimetre.

So she stayed motionless, putting a hand on Safiya's arm in an effort to reassure her—or maybe herself.

The muffled crunch of footsteps was coming nearer.

Mr. Morgan?

Sonnebourne?

The figure that finally moved into view, silvered by the moonlight, was neither of those. It was an Egyptian, a big, swarthy man Zoe thought she recognised as one of the crew on Sonnebourne's boat, although she hadn't been out of her cabin enough to get a good look at any of the sailors.

He wore a turban and a dark blue robe with an embroidered over-vest—and he was evidently very proud of the revolver he was holding. He kept tapping it against the open palm of his hand and smiling to himself. Zoe caught the flash of white teeth in the shadow of his face.

Holmes's tackle caught him completely off-guard; as the Egyptian man moved past, Holmes sprang at him from behind the column.

A smaller man would have been carried to the ground, but the Egyptian was heavyset enough that he only stumbled, off-balance, then swung the gun wildly in Holmes's direction.

Zoe heard the crack of a shot and the sound of the bullet ricocheting off stone before Holmes dodged, spun, and caught the attacker with an uppercut to the jaw.

The Egyptian man's head snapped back with the force of the blow, and he staggered, reeling backwards.

Zoe hadn't fully realised it until this moment, but the two of them were on the brink of a rocky precipice where the ground dropped away sharply to the river below. For an instant that seemed to stretch on and on, the heavyset man teetered on the edge, his arms flailing wildly.

Then he lost his balance and fell.

Zoe heard a sickening thud as his body struck the rocks on the shoreline below.

She ran towards Holmes, but he was already in motion, going to look over the edge.

"Dead," Holmes pronounced. "His head must have struck the rocks."

Zoe wouldn't have needed Holmes's confirmation; a glance was enough to tell her that the attacker hadn't survived the fall. He lay with his arms and legs twisted at awkward angles, eyes staring sightlessly up at the clear night sky.

"He is dead?" Safiya had come up to join them and now

spoke, her voice high and frightened as she, too, peered down. "You killed him?"

"He would have killed me first, had I given him the chance. Come," Holmes said. "He appears to have been alone, but we cannot take the chance that there are not more searchers about. We need to move."

He led the way, cutting across the temple courtyard towards the spot where he must have moored his own boat.

"Are you all right?" she asked.

"Perfectly. I was mistaken about the possibility of arterial bleeding. It is a flesh wound, nothing more."

Holmes's voice was flat with assurance. Beneath the wadded-up cloth that he still held pressed against the bullet wound, his shoulders were rigid, his posture straight. But Zoe could tell his steps were increasingly dragging.

Safiya tugged on her sleeve as Holmes moved to push through the branches of a scraggy acacia bush that blocked their way.

"This friend of yours," she whispered. Her eyes were wide and frightened in the moonlight. "He killed that man. And yet this does not trouble him at all?"

She had spoken so softly that even Zoe barely heard, but Holmes had ears like a cat's and always had.

He answered without looking back. "I should be in the wrong profession if such events did occasion me distress," he said. "Now, the boat is directly ahead. I suggest we row across to the neighbouring island of Bigeh, where we may take stock of our position and either beg or buy what supplies we need to further our escape."

CHAPTER 27: FLYNN

Flynn jumped up and found himself staring at an elderly woman who was sitting up in the middle of her bed. She had a wrinkled face with white hair that stood up in a kind of halo all around her head, and she was watching him with bright, interested eyes.

"Well, I must say that you look a trifle young to be Saint Nicholas," she said. "And rather small. Although I suppose he is described as *a right jolly old elf*, which of course implies that he would be of diminutive stature. How I loved that poem when I was young!" She beamed. "*'Twas the night before Christmas, and all through the house...* My papa used to read it to us every Christmas Eve. I believe that this, though, is December the 23rd. Or have I got my dates wrong?"

She put her head on one side in a way that reminded Flynn of a bird eyeing a worm, and gave him a critical stare.

"In any case, I must say you certainly don't look as though your belly would shake when you laugh like a bowl full of jelly. You're quite thin!"

"Ah, well ..." Flynn couldn't ever remember a time when he'd had less of an idea of what to say than he had now.

The old woman was talking to him all right, but something

in her bright eyes reminded him of Old Margaret, the beggar woman he knew who lived under Southwark Bridge. Mad as a hatter, Old Margaret was.

Becky put her head in through the window. "What are you—"

She stopped, her mouth dropping open at the sight of the old woman in the bed.

"She thinks we might be Saint Nicholas," Flynn said.

"We're his assistants," Becky said. She hopped down from the window sill.

"Are you really?" the old woman gave then another look of bright interest. "Then perhaps you can tell me something that I have always wanted to know about the reindeer—"

Flynn didn't hear whatever it was she wanted to know. Some thoughts snuck up on you slowly; others hit you all at once, like a ton of bricks—and the one that had just struck him was the second kind, practically slapping him in the face.

"They're planning to bomb Parliament!" he gasped.

Becky stopped whatever story she'd been making up about reindeer and stared at him. "What?"

"Farooq and the Sons of Ra. They're going to plant the bomb in Parliament. There's been an emergency session called, on account of the war in South Africa—it's all over the papers. And I overheard Farooq say something about Parliament when he was talking to the other man. And the Palace of Westminster—you said Jack had been called out on account of one of the guards there had been murdered. That's the building where Parliament meets: The Palace of Westminster. They probably killed the guard so that someone else—one of their lot—could take his place."

Becky's eyes had gone wide.

He turned to the old woman in the bed. "I don't suppose you know whether any new patients have been brought in here? Or where their rooms might be?"

From the look Becky shot him, she thought he'd be more likely to find tiny reindeer up on the sanatorium roof than get any helpful information here. But the old woman nodded.

"Oh yes, indeed. Someone was brought in just this evening. I heard them talking out in the hall. Dr. Harrison—such a nice man, he's the one who looks after me—was speaking to someone else, saying he wasn't happy about accepting a private patient, especially with whoever it was insisting that the patient would only be seen by their own special doctor, no one else and no one on the staff here. But then the other man said that he would pay Dr. Harrison twice what he usually charged for a patient's care here, and that it would only be for a day or two. And Dr. Harrison said all right, and they could have room 205. That's at the end of the hall," she added. "Near the stair case."

"Thank you!" Becky said.

"You're quite welcome." The elderly woman inclined her head in a regal sort of nod. "I confess that I don't quite see what bombs and Parliament have to do with Christmas and the reindeer, but I am glad to have been of service. Do come again, if Saint Nicholas will permit it. I have no chimney in here as you see, but you would be quite welcome to come in through the window as you did tonight."

* * *

They peered out into the hall cautiously, but it was empty, probably because at this time of the evening most of the residents who could be up and about were downstairs having dinner.

The place didn't feel like a hospital to Flynn; it was more like a fancy kind of house, with gas lights in brass sconces along the walls and thick carpets on the floor.

The carpets at least made it easier to move quietly. Together, he and Becky tiptoed to the end of the corridor to a door marked with a brass plaque that was etched with the number 5.

Flynn put his ear close to the wood panel, and then jumped because a voice spoke on the other side.

"Where is your brother? Where is Sherlock Holmes?"

Flynn didn't recognise the voice, but he'd guess it belonged to the blond-haired man who'd driven the ambulance, the one who'd met with Farooq. He had an accent Flynn thought was German, and he must be talking to Mr. Mycroft.

No one answered, and the German tried again, his voice a deep growl. "There is no point in stalling, we will have the information out of you, eventually. You are quite at our mercy here, and the equipment I was allowed to carry in as a doctor contains several interesting surgical instruments that might loosen your tongue. I will kill you in the end, but I can assure you, I would have no scruples whatsoever in causing you a considerable degree of pain—"

"Stop!" Without thinking, Flynn burst through the door and tumbled into the room.

CHAPTER 28: ZOE

The floor of the hut was nothing but bare, dusty earth, and Zoe strongly suspected that the blanket she had been given was alive with fleas. But she was too exhausted and too chilled to care. She wrapped its folds around her and took a sip from the bowl of some sort of stew that one of the village women—dressed all in black, with her face veiled for modesty—had brought.

She wasn't sure exactly what story Holmes and Safiya had told between them to the village head man, who had come out to greet them on their arrival. As she might have expected, Holmes's command of Arabic was excellent, and whatever explanation he gave—or perhaps it was the handful of Egyptian bank notes he held out—had bought them an enthusiastic reception.

With almost dizzying speed, they were ushered into the head man's own hut—which unlike the other village dwellings had more than one room—and offered food, grass mats and blankets for sleeping, and cups of sweet mint tea.

A crowd of curious children had gathered to peer in at them—rather like visitors to the zoo looking in on a new and exotic breed of animal, Zoe thought. But they had giggled in response to whatever Holmes said to them, bobbed heads in thanks for the coins he distributed, and scampered away.

Now they were alone, the headman having apparently—as part of the price Holmes had paid in banknotes—agreed to vacate the premises for the remainder of the night. Safiya was lying in one corner of the room, curled up on her own grass mat and deep in a profoundly exhausted sleep.

A lamp with a round shade of pierced tinwork sat on the floor in the centre of the room, casting spangled-looking shadows on the wall and allowing Zoe to see the bone-deep weariness that etched Holmes's features, as well.

"I'd better take a look at your shoulder," she said.

Holmes opened his mouth.

She held up her finger for silence. "Now, you asked the headman to bring whatever passes for an alcoholic beverage in this place—I assume with the intent of using it to sterilise the wound." She gestured to some earthenware jugs that had been set down near Holmes's sleeping mat. "You were probably planning to take care of it once I'd fallen asleep, but it will be more efficient to take care of it now. And besides, I'll do a better job of it than you would, one-handed."

The edges of Holmes's mouth thinned, but he didn't protest as she unwound the makeshift bandage of Safiya's scarf.

He didn't speak, either, as she took up one of the pots and started to trickle the liquid inside—it smelled like very strong beer—across the bullet wound. The headman had also provided some rags, but she didn't trust their cleanliness enough to use them.

Holmes's fingers twitched as the alcohol touched the bullet wound's ragged edges, and he clenched his jaw so tightly that

Zoe wouldn't have been surprised to hear his teeth crack.

Zoe let out an exasperated breath. "You're allowed to make noise. I know it hurts."

"That will not be necessary."

"Of course not." She should have known better than to suggest such a thing. "What about telling me how you came to be in Egypt?"

"What is it that you wish to know?"

It was an old technique of Sherlock's, answering a question with one of his own—refusing to confide, not because there was any particular reason to conceal information, just because his habit of reticence was so ingrained as to be second nature to him.

Zoe stopped what she was doing and looked him square in the face, gritting her own teeth and spacing the words out. "You're trying to distract yourself from the pain. A few moments ago, you were playing mental chess openings—your fingers kept moving as if to track patterns of the pieces on the board. Now, you can either move on to translating Shakespeare into Hindustani or whatever other mental gymnastics you care to come up with. Or you can talk to me. Begin with Dr. Watson and Lucy. Are they all right?"

She held her breath as she waited for him to answer the question, even though she knew that if anything had happened to Lucy, he would have told her already.

Wouldn't he?

"They are both safe. So far as I know," Holmes amended. "They travelled straight to Aswan, where I assume they are now."

Zoe felt a knot of anxiety in her relax, at least a fraction.

"Good. Now, what is Sonnebourne planning? Do you know?"

"I've an inkling, yes. His ultimate goal—even beyond his work for the Kaiser—is to destabilise Britain's rule in Egypt. But as to how he plans to accomplish it—"

Holmes sucked in a sharp breath as Zoe wiped blood away from his wound with a clean edge of the scarf.

"I'm sorry," Zoe said. "I wish Dr. Watson were here to do this instead."

"You need not apologise. Discomfort is a necessary part of the process."

Holmes picked up the second jar of beer, though, and downed half of it in a single gulp. The pain must be even worse than Zoe had thought.

"Do you think it's wise for you to be drinking anything alcoholic?"

"Possibly not. But it most likely carries less risk than imbibing the local drinking water." Holmes set the jar down. The local brew must have indeed been strong, because the line of his mouth relaxed slightly. Then he asked, "Sonnebourne confided nothing to you that might hint of his plans?" he asked.

"Nothing except his extreme dislike—one might even say hatred—of you," Zoe said. She tried to ignore the cold that crawled through her at the memory of Sonnebourne's voice as he spoke Holmes's name. "He will kill you if he gets the chance."

"The feeling is entirely mutual." Holmes's gaze was fixed on the lighted lamp, and the muscles under Zoe's fingers were as hard as stone. "As to the second part of your statement, I do not intend to give him that chance. The village head man has a horse—his prize possession, but one he is willing to sell for the generous sum I have offered. The animal will carry only two of us, but our host knows of a man in a nearby village with a camel which he may be willing to sell. He has gone to make the necessary negotiations and will return before dawn, so that we may be away from here at first light."

Zoe nodded. Unless Sonnebourne or his men caught up with them first. She didn't say it, but the words hung unspoken in the smoke-tinged air.

"It will be all right." Holmes spoke no less stiffly than before, but the words were meant for an attempt at reassurance—one he probably wouldn't have made without the effects of the beer he'd drunk. She should probably accept them as such.

Zoe finished cleaning the bullet wound and, since there was nothing better at hand, re-wrapped the scarf around it.

"How does that feel?" she asked.

Holmes had relaxed a little, leaning his head against the mud-brick wall behind him, his eyes half-closed. The lamplight picked out the hard intelligence of his features, the way a trickle of perspiration had streaked his brow and bare throat.

"Have you fallen asleep?" Zoe asked when he didn't answer.

"I'm merely contemplating how to reply," Holmes regarded her from under half-lowered lids. "The last time I attempted to give you a report on my physical condition, you threatened me with grievous bodily harm if not murder."

Zoe laughed before she could stop herself. Holmes was smiling, as well—actually smiling, and her heart contracted with a pang that was half pleasure, half pain.

She had almost never seen him as he was now, laughing and unguarded. Something else he would never have permitted himself to be, if not for the combined effects of pain, alcohol, and blood loss. But this Sherlock Holmes was far harder to cope with—and far more dangerous to her peace of mind—than the coldly rational thinking machine.

Before Zoe could answer, the door to the hut burst open, and one of the village men appeared, panting and speaking in a flood of desperate-sounding Arabic.

Cold lodged in Zoe's heart like a knife-sharp shard of ice, and she knew even before Holmes turned to her to translate what he was about to say.

"The headman assigned this man and some others to keep watch on the riverbank, and they've just spotted a large boat— a *dahabeeyah* of the kind hired by *Englezi*—heading this way, clearly intending to drop anchor and come ashore."

CHAPTER 29: FLYNN

Mr. Mycroft was on a bed—handcuffed to it, Flynn could see—with one arm all done up in bandages.

The German was standing over him, but he'd been so shocked by Flynn's entrance that he'd straightened up.

He was still holding a wickedly sharp-looking scalpel, though, and he had a gun on the table nearby, too. Still staring at Flynn, he made a grab for the gun.

Flynn jumped back, almost crashing into Becky, who was standing in the doorway with her face gone completely white, staring at him as if he'd gone completely off his head.

He couldn't blame her. Usually he was the one trying to stop her from jumping straight into danger without thinking. He couldn't have just stayed outside and let the German blighter hurt Mr. Mycroft, but he had to admit he hadn't any ideas for how to stop him, either. Right now, staring into the barrel of the German's gun, his head felt like a big, empty cupboard, bare of anything but cobwebs inside.

Becky was the first to find her voice. "You might as well give up," she said. "The police are right downstairs, they'll be here to arrest you any minute."

It was a good effort, but the German didn't look like he believed it any more than Flynn did. His lip curled.

And then, from behind Becky, a whole flood of policemen in blue uniforms came streaming into the room.

Flynn was so stunned he couldn't even count them all, but some of them tackled the German, knocking the gun out of his hand and pinning him to the ground. Another one took care of freeing Mr. Mycroft from the handcuffs on the bed.

And another one picked Becky up in a hug.

"Jack! You got our message!"

"I certainly did." Jack looked a bit grim around the mouth. "Is Constable Polk all right?"

"He's got a concussion from the blow to the head he took, but he'll recover. Becky—"

Becky cut off what was probably going to be a lecture about the dangers of them having gone off in the first place.

"I know, we should never have left and I'm sorry, but Jack, listen! Farooq and the Sons of Ra? They're planning to bomb Parliament! Flynn and Selim found the ingredients for making nitro-glycerin, but we don't know where they're keeping the bomb—"

"I believe that I may be able to help with that."

The voice was Mycroft's, speaking for the first time. He looked a bit off-colour, and the bullet wound had to be hurting him, but he spoke quite calmly. He was Mr. Holmes's brother, Flynn thought, and it took more than being shot and kidnapped to rattle Mr. Holmes. Either Mr. Holmes.

"Fortunately, our German friend here had not yet got around to making a search of my pockets." He nodded to the blond man, who was now wearing the handcuffs they'd taken off Mycroft, and looking daggers at the policemen holding him. "A careless oversight, but it means that I am able to give you the message I received this morning from Sherlock."

He drew a folded paper out of his inner waistcoat pocket, opened it, and read aloud.

"Strongly suspect Sonnebourne's organisation is using the townhome belonging to Paul Archer, number 26 Park Crescent."

CHAPTER 30: ZOE

Safiya sat up, her face blanched with terror, her eyes still dazed.

"What is it? What is happening?"

Holmes answered, his tone surprisingly gentle. "Safiya, I am afraid that we must assume Lord Sonnebourne is aware of your true identity. Or rather, your father's true identity."

"True identity?" Zoe repeated. "What do you mean? Didn't you tell me back in London that she came from an Egyptian village near Cairo, where her father was—"

Holmes shook his head. "That may be true, but it is not the whole truth." He turned to Safiya, and continued, "Is it."

He didn't make the words sound like a question, but Safiya bowed her head in acquiescence.

"It was the story our father told us—my brother and me—to give anyone in England who might ask where we came from. Although not many asked." Her mouth quirked briefly. "To most English persons, one foreigner is like another. But my father feared that we—and he—might be in danger if the truth were known. There are always unscrupulous men who would try to trade on my father's affection for us, to try to influence him—"

"Men such as Lord Sonnebourne." Holmes expression hard-ened.

"I don't understand," Zoe said. "Who is her father?"

"I had already reached the conclusion that she must have some sort of political value," Holmes said. "Otherwise, Son-nebourne's taking the trouble to bring her all this way into Egypt would be illogical in the extreme. However, it was not until this morning, when I received the telegram I mentioned before from Becky and Flynn, that I was able to prove my theory correct." He looked at Safiya and said, still speaking with uncharacteristic gentleness. "The message contained a name. That of Ahmed Urabi."

Safiya sat with her head still bowed, and was silent so long that at first Zoe thought she wasn't going to answer. But then she said, her voice soft, "He was—is—my father's greatest friend. They joined the army together."

"Then Ahmed Urabi rose to the rank of colonel," Holmes said. "Due to his humble roots, he came to be viewed by many as the authentic voice of people of Egypt. He represented a peasant population who had grown resentful of being ruled by tax-exempt foreigners and wealthy local landlords. Urabi com-manded the respect and support of not only the populace at large, but also a large portion of the Egyptian army as well. Re-volts led by 'Urabi's army spread across Egypt. Britain feared that if he succeeded in winning independence for his nation, Urabi would default on Egypt's massive debt and that he might try to gain control of the Suez Canal. He was ultimately de-feated, captured, and exiled to Ceylon. But I would imagine that he remains a popular name amongst the native Egyptian members of the Egyptian army, who all too often are given their orders by British officers who consider them inherently inferior."

Safiya nodded acknowledgment, her lips tightly compressed.

"I would also imagine"—Holmes went on—"that your father, as a close personal friend of 'Urabi's, is also a popular figure, commanding a huge degree of respect among the men?"

"My father also has risen to the rank of colonel." Safiya's voice was so low it was almost a whisper. "He even hopes one day that he might win 'Urabi's freedom, bring enough pressure to bear on Khedive Abbas II that he might allow 'Urabi to return to Egypt."

"A worthy goal," Holmes said. "However, what is more to the point is the fact that Sonnebourne evidently views you as an effective bargaining chip. He planned to hold you as hostage to your father's compliance with his schemes—threatening your life unless your father agrees to lead the army in a revolt against their British officers. An act which, however justified, would result in an extreme loss of life—and would ultimately place the entire force of the Egyptian army under Sonnebourne's control, with your father as a puppet commander only."

Safiya looked desperately frightened, but she clasped her hands tightly together and nodded.

"You must get her away from here," Zoe said. In her mind's eye, she was calculating the amount of time it would take Sonnebourne's boat to navigate the rocks around the island, find a place to drop anchor, and come ashore. Surely not long enough.

"It's the only way we have of stopping Sonnebourne's plan," she said. "The village head man's horse—"

"Will carry only two people," Holmes said.

"I know. So you said. And failing the miraculous arrival of the head man with the camel he promised, I can see only one option: you take Safiya—"

"No."

Zoe ignored the interruption. "It's our best chance—"

"I refuse to leave you behind."

Holmes looked desperately exhausted, with lines of strain bracketing his mouth and his eyes dulled by pain or alcohol or both. But his voice was curt, and he was giving her the kind of coldly furious look that usually made even strong men wilt and women start to cry.

Zoe glared back at him. "We haven't the time to argue!" she snapped. "You're the one who's always speaking of logic and reason. You're in no condition to fight, therefore we can't stay here. Therefore, the only logical course of action is for you and Safiya to go on horseback—"

"I said no!"

Zoe stared. She'd seldom seen Holmes's iron control slip, but he sounded as close to losing his temper as she could remember.

"On what grounds?" she demanded. "I can't go with Safiya. I don't speak any Arabic, and two women travelling alone would stand out. We'd be seen and recaptured before we'd gone more than a mile. You do speak Arabic; in disguise you can blend in—pass Safiya off as your daughter, especially if she borrows one of those black robes and veils from one of the village women. Her life is worth more than mine—"

"Not to me!" Holmes voice was a ragged shout.

Then he stopped, breathing hard, looking as though he were half-relieved, half-appalled by the words that had just come from his mouth.

That made two of them.

"I … thank you," she stammered. Impossible man. He would choose *now* to speak, when there was every chance that she might never see him again. Zoe pressed her eyes shut against a sting of tears, then forced herself to smile.

"I will remember that," she said softly. "Go now, with Safiya. I'll be all right. I'm sure the villagers will be willing to hide me, especially if you give them another generous payment for services rendered. All I have to do is crouch in the shadows, disguised as one of the village women, while they swear that no *Englezi* have come anywhere near here."

If he hadn't been exhausted, weakened from blood loss, and in pain, Holmes probably wouldn't have thought that it could possibly work out as Zoe had said. But as it was, she managed to see him and Safiya—well-wrapped in a borrowed robe and veil—loaded onto the back of the newly purchased horse, which they had led to the edge of the village.

Once at the far end of the island, a ferry would take them across to the West Bank of the Nile.

A narrow strip of rosy-pearl dawn was just breaking at the edge of the horizon, turning the eastern mountains lavender-purple when they rode away. Holmes turned just once to look at her over his shoulder. He raised his hand in farewell, then rode away.

Zoe let out her breath and turned back to the village, hurrying along the narrow dirt lane back towards the head man's hut.

She was halfway there when she heard the unmistakable crack of a gunshot.

"That was a warning!" She recognised the voice as Morgan's, though it was so choked with fury that the words were scarcely intelligible. "Tell me where the woman is, or I will shoot your people, one by one. Starting with this disgusting child here!"

A woman's high, terrified scream accompanied the last words—probably the child's mother.

The substance in Zoe's lungs felt more like hot glue than air, but she forced herself to draw a steadying breath, then walked out of her hiding place to where Morgan stood on the edge of the riverbank.

The carefully groomed Englishman was entirely transformed. He looked half-deranged, with his face flushed and twisted with anger, his hair rumpled and his clothes dishevelled.

Sonnebourne must have rousted him out of bed and threatened him with dire consequences if she, Zoe, was not found.

"That won't be necessary," Zoe said steadily.

The child Morgan had threatened—a little boy—was cowering on the ground, his mother beside him with her arms thrown protectively over him.

"Put the gun away, Mr. Morgan," Zoe said. "I will come with you quite willingly."

CHAPTER 31: WATSON

At dawn the next morning, December 24, I was awakened by a persistent rapping at my hotel room door. At the moment, the rooms of the Old Cataract hotel were nearly all taken by managers, supervisors, vendors and tradesmen working on their respective aspects of the vast dam construction project, though one day, when the dam was complete, the management fully expected to fill the hotel with tourists. Our rooms were on the top floor. We had no view of the river, for our travel arrangements, with an eye to economy, had necessitated choosing the less-expensive eastern side. Nonetheless, my bed and sitting rooms were both comfortably furnished and already illuminated by the golden glow of the beginning sunrise.

I opened my door and beheld Lucy, already dressed and holding what appeared to be a hand-written note.

"It's a message from Holmes," she said. "It arrived during the night."

She handed the folded paper—which was little more than a ragged scrap that appeared to have been torn from some wrapping material—over to me. I read the brief message.

Lucy, proceed to the Aswan dam construction site, where if all goes well, I shall join you. Watson, I pray you will remain at the hotel. In particular, keep watch on the lobby. —S.H.

"At least we know that he is alive, and able to issue communication."

"True." Lucy was frowning, though, her expression worried. "Look here, though." She pointed to where there were a few smudges of rusty red on the edge of the message. "Blood, do you think?"

I would have liked to offer reassurance but could not. Lucy would not have believed in empty platitudes.

"Holmes is alive," I repeated. "And it seems to me the best way that we can assist him is to do as he asks."

Lucy nodded. "I will hire a guide and a donkey and go to the dam construction." She smiled briefly. "I wonder what Lord Kitchener will think when I turn up again—probably that I'm a frightful nuisance."

"If that is all Lord Kitchener has to complain of by the end of today, I will be heartily thankful."

"So will I," Lucy said soberly.

CHAPTER 32: ZOE

"Here she is." Morgan gave Zoe a shove up the final steps leading to the upper deck of the boat.

It was the only time he had touched her on the journey. From his expression, he would have liked to cause her significantly more harm than a simple push to the shoulder. But Sonnebourne must have given orders that she was to be unharmed.

"Thank you," Sonnebourne said.

Sonnebourne stood at the rail of the boat, apparently deep in contemplation of the sunrise now showing over the eastern mountains.

In the distance, to both the right and left of the river, rose long ranges of yellow limestone mountains, the natural crevices in the landscape painted with violet and blue shadows by the early morning sun.

He turned and glanced at Morgan.

"Leave us."

Morgan looked as though he would have liked to argue, but obeyed, vanishing down the steps to the lower deck.

Sonnebourne still faced the rising sun and was silent. "Have you ever heard the story of Osiris?"

Zoe had braced herself for interrogation—torture, even—as he sought to find out where Holmes had gone.

She blinked at the question. "No."

"He was one of many gods worshiped here in Egypt, in ancient times. The story goes that he was murdered by his jealous brother Set. Set cut up Osiris's body and hid parts of it all over Egypt, up and down the river Nile. But Osiris's faithful wife, Isis, searched for Osiris' remains and reassembled his body and restored him to life."

Sonnebourne tilted his face up, as though better to catch the breeze of the river and the sun's rays. "Osiris's death and triumphant resurrection were said to be reenacted daily in the rising and setting of the sun. On the day of the winter solstice, the ancient Egyptians celebrated by decorating their homes with leaves from the date palm tree. The green of the leaves was believed to signify immortality, the eternal triumph of life over death."

Zoe's skin prickled. Not since Professor James Moriarty could she remember fearing and disliking a man as much as she did Lord Sonnebourne. And yet somehow, as he spoke, the intensity of his voice seemed to turn back the hands of time, scrolling through the centuries until she could almost imagine them back in those ancient days.

A farmer, wearing nothing but a simple white loincloth, stood on the edge of the nearby river bank. He was using a shâdûf to draw up water for his crops, while behind him a team of oxen ploughed the fields. Just as they would have done six thousand years ago.

"Look around you!" Sonnebourne swept a hand out towards the river, the fields of cultivation, and the desert mountains beyond. "This country was great, once! A mighty nation, capable of conquest, ruled by Pharaohs who raised monuments the like of which the world has never seen since. Under the rule of the Turks and now the English, it has fallen into decay. But it could rise and become mighty once again."

"Like Osiris, rising from the dead?"

"Exactly like!" Sonnebourne's voice throbbed, and something fanatical flashed in his blue gaze. "We had no time to stop at Thebes on our journey. If we had, I would have shown you the temple of Medinet Habu, where pharaoh Ramses III inscribed the story of his triumph over foreign armies on the walls: *Those who came on land were overthrown and slaughtered … Amon-Re was after them destroying them. Those who entered the river mouths were like birds ensnared in the net … their leaders were carried off and slain. They were thrown down and pinioned …*"

His voice caressed the words, lingering. His eyes had gone flat and distant, and his lips curved in a remote smile that made ice crystals form under Zoe's skin, despite the heat of the sun.

"And you plan to become another Ramses?" she asked.

"Ramses?" Sonnebourne threw back his head again and laughed. "Why would I aim so low? Ramses and all the pharaohs like him are dead and dust, now, their temples and monuments in ruins, their tombs torn apart by grave robbers, their treasures gone. I will be another Osiris."

He stopped. "Shall I tell you how it will be? Look, you can see the dam construction from here."

He gestured to the great earthen barrier upstream of the main construction site. On the barrier, two huge steam shovels and two gigantic steam cranes stood silent, their huge buckets hanging empty over the earthen surface, suspended by steel cables.

"The work will halt at the end of the day, so that the Christians among the work crew may celebrate the holiday tomorrow," Sonnebourne said. "My confederate amongst the work crews has already hidden the detonator and the charges. I assume you overheard at least some of our meeting on Philae?"

There seemed no point in denying it, so Zoe nodded.

"I shall go to the construction site this afternoon wearing the uniform of an Egyptian Army officer and claim to be making an inspection of the work's progress," Sonnebourne went on. "That will get me past the guards who remain on duty. On the earthen bank you can see up there in the distance will be a pile of straw and dirt. Directly beneath the dirty straw will be a detonator. When the plunger is depressed, a timer will be activated, and eventually a switch will turn, completing an electrical circuit that will send current down wires within three long pipes, each stuffed with dynamite. The pipes are buried within the earthen wall, and they run in the downstream direction all the way across to the construction side. The explosion will breach the entire width of the earthen barrier."

"And once you have pleased your German masters by murdering thousands of innocent people and undermining Britain's control of Egypt, they will reward you by granting you rulership of the country, when they are the conquerors here?"

Instead of answering, Sonnebourne smiled, a slow, lazy smile, and stretched out a hand. "Every Osiris must have his Isis."

"And you are inviting me to fulfill that role?" Zoe knew she ought to summon up a flattered smile, try to persuade Sonnebourne that she was considering the offer.

She couldn't manage it.

Sonnebourne, reading her expression, sighed. "A pity. We

should have made a fine king and queen, you and I." He raised his voice. "Morgan?"

The barrister must have been standing just out of sight, because his head appeared almost at once at the top of the stairs.

"Take her below," Sonnebourne said. "Tell Olfrig to tie her up with the other one, then get ready to accompany me to the site of the dam. We must not be late for our appointment with destiny."

CHAPTER 33: WATSON

I was dressing in haste, making ready to proceed to the hotel lobby as Holmes had asked. I heard a knock at my door. Expecting Lucy, I opened it. But instead I saw a dark-complexioned young woman, dressed in the uniform of an Egyptian hotel maid.

"Dr. Watson?"

"I am."

"I have been asked to bring you at once. A medical emergency. Mr. Paul Archer."

"Archer is here? I had thought him in Cairo."

She bobbed her head. "He is in great distress and asked for you to come at once. A matter of life and death."

I hesitated. To have a call for help from Archer come at this moment, when I was obeying Holmes's request and could ill afford to leave my post, set my heart racing.

But if Archer was in danger—

I studied the girl's face. She appeared desperately in earnest, her wide eyes imploring beneath the fringe of her white cotton head scarf.

"Where?" I asked.

"The motorized felucca *Chimera*. She is moored at the hotel dock just at the base of the cliff. I am to take you there, if you will come."

I debated only a moment more before making my choice.

"I will come. Just let me fetch my medical kit."

I found my medical bag and followed her, my heart rate quickening.

Finally we were on the embankment at the edge of the great river, and then on the wooden dock. The fourth ship along the dock was the *Chimera*, and a gangplank led from the dock onto the deck.

From inside the cabin came a cry of pain. I recognized Paul's voice.

I pressed a pound note into the hand of the maid, hurried to the gangplank, and came on board.

The bulkhead door leading to the cabin was open.

I called out, trying to see inside the cabin. "Paul?"

There seemed to be several people seated in the darkness within. I could not make out their features.

Then I felt a gun press into the small of my back. At the same moment, an electric torch was lit within the cabin.

Behind me I heard a woman's voice. "Remember me, Doctor? Little April Norman? Paul's faithful assistant at the London Zoo?"

I turned and saw her, now without the scarf that had concealed her hair. She had darkened her complexion with some cosmetic to appear Egyptian. And she held a pistol trained on my heart.

"You were charged with murder and embezzlement. You were convicted and imprisoned," I said.

"Only for embezzlement. And released after a modest stay in prison," she said. "Lord Sonnebourne provided the services of Mr. Morgan, an excellent barrister. And a position as Mr. Morgan's housekeeper. I'm now the very respectable Mrs. Orles, and soon I will be mistress of Paul Archer's townhouse in Regent's Park. Now come inside and meet your other friends."

In the light of the electric torch, I saw Archer and Zoe seated on the floor of the small cabin. Both were bound and gagged with white handkerchiefs.

Beside Zoe stood Olfrig. He was holding a pistol clapped to Zoe's temple.

Olfrig gave a triumphant smile. "Ah, Dr. Watson. We meet again. It is fortunate that you were in your room when Miss Norman arrived."

Then his expression hardened. "Where is Holmes?"

Cold fury surged through my veins. Olfrig, his beady eyes bright behind his spectacles, was watching me with great interest, the way an experimenter watches a rat in a maze.

He was attempting to disconcert me, to evoke the sense of powerlessness I must have had when he had drugged me at his Homburg spa clinic.

"Holmes is dead," I said. "As I told you when we met in Cairo."

"You lie," said Olfrig. He placed the muzzle of his pistol beneath Zoe's chin, causing her to turn her head aside. Above the white cloth that prevented her from speaking, her eyes were wide with fear and anger. "He secured the rescue of another of Lord Sonnebourne's guests only last night."

I could not suppress a slight start of shock at the news. Holmes had rescued Safiya. It must be Safiya to whom Olfrig referred.

I glanced at Zoe, and she gave an infinitesimal nod of confirmation, as though reading my thoughts.

Beside her, Archer looked glassy-eyed with terror.

"Remove Miss Rosario's gag," I said.

"Where is Holmes?" Olfrig repeated.

I knew I had information that Olfrig wanted. Otherwise he would have shot me. "Remove the gag and I will talk," I said.

"You are in no position to bargain."

"Then shoot me. If you dare. You know the authorities will hear."

"Close the cabin door, Miss Norman," Olfrig said.

I folded my arms across my chest.

Olfrig appeared thoughtful. "You appeared surprised at what I told you about Holmes's courageous movements last night. Which leads me to ask myself whether you really have any vital information?"

"You might try drugging me again," I said. "But you would have to shoot me first."

Olfrig aimed his pistol at me as his free hand reached out to undo the knotted cloth at the back of Zoe's neck.

I hurled myself at him, downwards and forwards, still with my arms crossed, crashing into Olfrig just above his ankles. He shot wildly as he went down. The bullet missed. I landed on my right shoulder and rolled past him, drawing my pistol from my left coat pocket as I came upright.

He shot again while scrambling to his knees. His bullet grazed my arm.

Lying on my back, I saw him above me, getting his balance and aiming his pistol for a third shot.

I fired.

My bullet hit him below his jaw. It went straight up through his brain and exited in a shower of red through the top of his skull.

I turned and saw Miss Norman at the doorway. She was bent over, mouth agape, gasping as though about to be sick, staring in horror at the fallen Olfrig.

Her pistol dangled at her side.

"You should have taken more care to make sure that I was unarmed, Miss Norman," I said. "I recognized you at once, even in Egyptian disguise, and took the precaution of pocketing my revolver when I went to fetch my medical kit. Another oversight of yours. But then, overweening confidence always was your downfall. Now, drop your weapon."

Instead of doing as I ordered, she straightened, lips compressed, face hardened with determination, bringing her pistol to bear on me.

As she fired, I shot her between the eyes.

* * *

I removed the gags from Zoe and Archer.

Archer's gaze was fixed on April Norman's crumpled body as I removed his gag. He continued to stare at her while he got his breath.

Then he said, "She taunted me. They never intended to fund my research. It was only a ruse, to make me go to Egypt, where I would conveniently vanish. The papers I signed for the venture were used to forge a document giving her power of attorney to manage all my affairs in my absence. They were going to kill me here, and she was going to return to London and occupy my town house in Park Crescent."

"A devil's plan," I said. "No doubt Sonnebourne was behind it."

Zoe said, "There are knives in the galley."

I found one and used it to cut the cords that bound their hands and feet.

"Where is Holmes?" Zoe was already on her feet. "And where is Lucy?"

"Lucy is at the dam construction site, by Holmes's request. As for Holmes, I can only hope that he has joined her."

Zoe bit her lip. "He was wounded last night—shot—but we must hurry. Sonnebourne and Morgan are already making for the construction site, as well. They plan … But there isn't time to explain. We must go there at once!"

CHAPTER 34: WATSON

I raced up the path towards the construction site. Zoe, exhausted by her ordeal, had fallen behind, but when I would have helped her, she had waved me to go on.

"Sonnebourne's men have buried dynamite! He will detonate it and blow up the dam!"

I reached the top of the path, where a wooden fence separated me from the earthen barrier. At the gate within the fence stood a British soldier, holding an Enfield rifle, conversing with another man wearing the garb of one of the native workers.

"There is danger!" I gasped. "You must report to Kitchener—"

I got no further. The native workman turned, revealing Holmes's familiar countenance.

He grasped my hand in greeting, with a motion for silence.

"Kitchener has already been warned, thanks to Lucy," he said. "But Sonnebourne must be caught in the act. He is a powerful man, and has allies even yet amid the British government. If he is to be utterly defeated, we must have proof of his crimes."

Together, we slipped through the gate in the wooden fence. Holmes led the way behind one of the huge construction cranes. I followed. We went on for a few more paces, till we were behind another crane. Far below us on our left I could see hundreds of construction workers moving into formation, as though preparing to leave their work at the end of the day.

Holmes tapped my shoulder and pointed in the opposite direction, towards the earthen barrier that protected the construction site from the flow of the great river.

My heart thudded as I beheld Sonnebourne, wearing the uniform of an army officer. A few paces behind him was the barrister Morgan, also in uniform. They were approaching the edge of the barrier, where the enormous man-made mountain of earth began its gradual downward slope to the water.

Sonnebourne eased his large frame over the edge and down the slope a few paces. He crouched like a fencer, one leg outwards for balance, as he reached down to push away a pile of dirty straw.

The straw fluttered down the sand-coloured slope.

"Sonnebourne!" Holmes's voice cracked like a whip. "You are under arrest. You are surrounded. Surrender now and keep your life."

I could see the big man clearly. Holmes and I were emerging into his field of view, coming out from behind the second construction crane.

Sonnebourne spun around. His face was a mask of rage. "I'll see you dead first," he said. He reached for the detonator he had just exposed with one hand. His other hand held a pistol. He raised the pistol and fired.

I returned fire. As did Holmes.

Sonnebourne staggered towards us, bleeding, but still moving, pistol wavering, then steadying as he aimed at Holmes.

We fired again, in unison. Sonnebourne's khaki-uniformed

chest now had a dark round bloodstain spreading out beneath the collection of false medals. He crumpled to the ground.

Behind him, the barrister Morgan went to his knees, dropping his own pistol, his empty hands upraised in surrender.

Kitchener and four army riflemen stepped from behind the nearby steam shovel. "A close one, Mr. Holmes," Kitchener said. "But you called it exactly. Some day you must tell us how you reasoned it all out."

"Thank you for allowing us to do this ourselves," Holmes replied.

We stood over the fallen Sonnebourne. The huge body that had caused so much suffering over so many years now lay prostrate.

But his hand still held the pistol. It moved, ever so slightly.

Holmes stamped down on it hard. Finger bones cracked. Sonnebourne cried out once. Then a shudder went through his massive frame. He lay still.

Holmes kicked the pistol away.

I knelt and pressed my fingertips to his neck, just below the ear. There was no pulse. He was dead.

Morgan, only a few feet away, called out, "Gentlemen!"

"You have been caught red-handed," Kitchener said, his voice dripping with contempt, "in a flagrant act of treason."

"I am a barrister in the court of Her Majesty the Queen in London," Morgan said. "I was acting under duress. I claim my rights as a British citizen under due process. I intend to establish ..."

His voice trailed off as he saw Kitchener nod to the four riflemen. They aimed their weapons.

"No!" cried Morgan.

Kitchener nodded again.

Four rifles spoke. On its knees, Morgan's body seemed to dance for a moment as the bullets hit.

Then it collapsed.

"There is a time for due process," Kitchener said as the four soldiers dragged away the bodies. "This wasn't it."

Then he added, "By the way, our men found the *Chimera*, that boat you thought was being used by Sonnebourne. Two bodies were discovered on board. A young British woman and an older German man. It appears they had a falling out and shot each other."

CHAPTER 35: WATSON

A few hours later, Holmes, Zoe, and I entered the lobby of the Grand Cataract Hotel. I saw Lucy immediately, on the far side of the room nearest the entry door. She was partially concealed by the base of the entry partition, one of the peculiarly Egyptian striped arches that curve inward at the bottom, like the Greek letter omega. She wore her usual black suit. A black straw hat shaded her lovely face as she kept her eyes downwards, apparently focused on something she was knitting out of dark green wool.

She looked up immediately, saw Zoe with us, and gave us a radiant smile of joy and relief. A moment later she was with us, hugging Zoe.

"So you're back," she said. "Did everything go well?"

"I'm proof of that," Zoe said. "But your father has a bit of an injury. Though he won't admit it's of any importance."

Holmes tapped his wounded shoulder. "It isn't," he said.

"I have some news myself," Lucy said. "Coincidentally, Mycroft also has a wounded shoulder." She took two telegraph messages from her reticule and handed one over to Holmes. "This is his telegram. Flynn and Becky rescued him. Later Jack and his men found nitroglycerine stored at Paul Archer's town house in Regent's Park."

Holmes was reading the message. "And they arrested a German who had abducted Mycroft. Possible confirmation of the Kaiser's involvement with Sonnebourne." Then he looked up. "But Mycroft says nothing of having been wounded."

"Well, Mycroft wouldn't, would he?" Lucy replied. "That bit of news is in this other telegram. It's from Jack." She folded that message and put it back in her reticule. Her eyes were shining. "He says Flynn and Becky were heroes. By the way, how soon can we go back to London?"

CHAPTER 36: WATSON

Kitchener said, "Now, Mr. Holmes. You promised to tell me how you reasoned it out."

It was noon the next day. In the dining hall of the Aswan British Army barracks, a festive Christmas banquet had just concluded.

Holmes and I were still seated at the head table with Kitchener and several of his senior officers. Around us the tables were emptying. Two hundred British troops and nearly a hundred workmen who had wished to join the celebration were getting to their feet, heading for an auditorium in the same building, where entertainment was to be provided. The men were eager to reach their seats, for they had been told that not only would some of their talented comrades be performing, but also on stage would be the acclaimed London soprano, Lucy James.

Holmes put the tips of his fingers together and leaned back in his chair. His right arm was in a sling, but otherwise he looked none the worse for his injury. Dressed in impeccable white tie and tail coat, he would never have been recognized as the robed native workman who had stopped Sonnebourne's act of treason.

"Knowing the importance of the Aswan dam project," he

said, "I was certain there would be some attack there. Sonnebourne's plan was to orchestrate a bombing attempt on Parliament on the 23rd, timed so that he could take advantage of the resulting confusion in London and throughout the Empire. With Parliament threatened—and many of its members dead or wounded—Sonnebourne's path to wrest control of Egypt away from Britain would be significantly smoother."

"The bombing plot was foiled by Scotland Yard, I understand," said Kitchener. "I had a telegraph message to that effect this morning."

"As did we, I'm thankful to say," I put in. I did not mention the role played by Becky and Flynn. This was not the moment for lengthy explanation.

"I also understand," Kitchener went on, "that Sonnebourne planned to rally the Egyptian army to revolt, using an Egyptian, Colonel Asfour, as a figurehead."

"He was holding the colonel's daughter as his hostage," Holmes said. "We had met her on another case involving Sonnebourne, and we were aware of her kidnapping in London. We were fortunate enough to be able to help with her rescue here in Egypt."

Holmes did not elaborate, but I knew that, before journeying to the dam construction site, Holmes had seen Safiya reunited with her grateful father.

"However, you and your men deserve a great deal of the credit, milord," Holmes said to Kitchener. "For heeding our warnings without question, when they came, and for acting without delay when danger threatened."

Holmes has always been generous in giving credit when a case has been completed. And it was Christmas, after all.

* * *

Kitchener left us to join his men in the auditorium. Holmes and I lingered at the now-empty table. He appeared thoughtful, as if some part of the great puzzle we had undertaken still remained to be sorted out.

Finally, he said, "Let us go and hear Lucy."

As Holmes and I approached the auditorium, the entertainment had already begun. We could hear Lucy, singing in her beautiful, clear soprano. Entering, we saw her, standing at the center of the stage, dressed in black velvet, just as brilliantly radiant as the first time I had seen her, four years earlier, on the stage at the Savoy Theatre. Every man in the crowded audience seemed spellbound.

We continued to watch from the back, waiting until Lucy had concluded a Christmas carol and the audience burst into cheers. Amid their enthusiastic calls for an encore, Holmes and I walked quickly down the side aisle to find seats closer to the stage.

There we saw Zoe, seated in the front row, looking up at Lucy, clapping her hands in ardent applause. Dressed in black velvet, she was as lovely as her daughter.

I saw Holmes take a half step forward, as though about to take the empty seat beside her. Then he stopped and stood motionless.

I cleared my throat, uncertain whether I ought to say anything, but somehow driven to speak out nonetheless.

"You know, Holmes," I began, "despite the sorrow of bereavement, I have never for an instant regretted my marriage to Mary."

Holmes glanced at me, and favoured me with one of his brief

smiles. This one, I thought, was tinged with something that might have been regret.

Then he replied, "And no one was or is more deserving of domestic happiness than you, my old friend. However, the work I do—it is done so that others may be fortunate enough to have those happy, domestic lives if they so choose. Such a life for me was never part of the bargain."

I could say nothing, so I merely bowed my head.

But I noticed that Holmes moved to the chair beside Zoe's after all, and that his hand just brushed her shoulder as he sat down.

They looked at one another for a long moment, and then they looked up at Lucy, who had begun a new song.

"Silent night, holy night
All is calm, all is bright."

Both Holmes and Zoe smiled.

THE END

HISTORICAL NOTES

This is a work of fiction, and the authors make no claim that any of the historical locations or historical figures appearing in this story had even the remotest connection with the adventures recounted herein. However ...

1. The British Parliament generally adjourns in summer and does not return until the following February. But in 1899, there was a special session called late in December to address the need for military funding in South Africa. As far as the authors are aware, this session proceeded without incident.

2. Shepheard's Hotel in Cairo was one of the premier hospitality destinations in the world from the late nineteenth century until its destruction by fire in 1954. Dame Agatha Christie used it as a setting in her 1949 mystery novel, *Crooked House*.

3. The Old Cataract Hotel is still in operation in Aswan, now operating as The Sofitel Legend Old Cataract Hotel. Dame Agatha Christie used it as a setting for her 1937 mystery novel, *Death on the Nile*. The hotel also served as a location set for the 1978 film version of that famous story.

4. In 1902, the grounds of the temple complex on Philae Island were partially flooded when the Aswan low dam was put into

operation. The temple buildings sustained significant water damage in subsequent years. During the 1970s, the structures were taken down stone by stone and moved to their present location on higher ground at the nearby island of Agilkia, where they were rebuilt and restored. The move was part of the UNESCO restoration and preservation projects associated with construction of the Aswan High Dam, which went into operation approximately four miles upriver in 1970.

5. Field Marshal Horatio Herbert Kitchener, 1st Earl Kitchener, rose to become Secretary of War during WWI and was known for his somewhat ruthless and draconian policies. His face was immortalized on the WWI recruiting poster shown below. For his services protecting Egypt from Sudanese invaders, a grateful Egyptian government gave Kitchener a small personal island in the Nile, known as Kitchener's Island and today the site of the Aswan Botanical Garden. Kitchener also avidly practiced the craft of knitting. Millions of knitters today still utilize the Kitchener Stitch, a technique introduced in WWI to produce more durable socks for British soldiers. The stitch creates an apparently seamless toe.

6. The poem *A Visit from Saint Nicholas*, more commonly known as *'Twas the Night Before Christmas*, was first published anonymously in 1823 and later attributed to Clement Clarke Moore, who claimed authorship in 1837. Moore's connection with the poem has been questioned by those who use textual content analysis and external evidence to argue that Major Henry Livingston Jr., a New Yorker with Dutch and Scottish roots, should be considered the chief candidate for authorship, a view long espoused by the Livingston family.

7. While Safiya and her father are entirely fictional characters, Colonel Ahmed Urabi was an Egyptian patriot and national hero who led a revolt against British rule in Egypt as Holmes explained. Not long after the close of our story, in May 1901, 'Urabi was freed from exile and permitted to return to Egypt.

8. Lucy James will return.

A NOTE OF THANKS TO OUR READERS

Thank you for reading this Sherlock and Lucy story. We hope you've enjoyed it.

As you probably know, reviews make a big difference! So, we also hope you'll consider going back to the Amazon page where you bought the story and uploading a quick review. You can get to that page by using this link:

https://bit.ly/34fqaGU

You can also sign up for our mailing list to receive updates on new stories, special discounts, and 'free days' for some of our other books: www.SherlockandLucy.com

About the Authors

Anna Elliott is the author of the *Twilight of Avalon* trilogy, and *The Pride and Prejudice Chronicles*. She was delighted to lend a hand in giving the character of Lucy James her own voice, firstly because she loves Sherlock Holmes as much as her father, Charles Veley, and second because it almost never happens that someone with a dilemma shouts, "Quick, we need an author of historical fiction!" She lives in Pennsylvania with her husband and four children.

Charles Veley is the author of the first two books in this series of fresh Sherlock Holmes adventures. He is thrilled to be contributing Dr. Watson's chapters for the series, and delighted beyond words to be collaborating with Anna Elliott.

Made in the USA
Monee, IL
30 June 2023

38223464R00115